Vampire Hunter

Tobias Halson: Book One

John Evans

Cover Art Design by: Kelly Moran/Rowan Prose Publishing
Photo Credit: Adobe Images/Deposit Photos
First Edition
ISBN: 978-1-961967-48-9
Rowan Prose Publishing, LLC
www.RowanProsePublishing.com
Published in the United States of America

Praise for John Evans:

"A significant new voice in the genre."
-Entertainment Monthly

"Immersive and masterful."
-Bestselling Author Boris Bacic

Other works by John Evans:

"Man fears the darkness, and so he scrapes away at the edges of it with fire."
~ Rei Ayanami (Neon Genesis Evangelion)

Chapter 1

My name is Tobias Halson, and I'm a Vampire Hunter. No, seriously, I am. That's why I was chasing a dirty redneck down one of Philly's darker and smellier alleyways with an ax. Don't laugh, I'm not kidding. A lot of people have preconceived notions about how vampires are supposed to look and act, mainly from bad fiction and even worse movies. They are not the deeply misunderstood brooders of Anne Rice, the black-clothed pale makeup-wearing Goths, and they are especially not the lame glittering poofs from those god-awful movies.

I hate those things. They give people the wrong ideas about vampires and either get themselves killed or turned, make my job harder or, worst case scenario, get *me* killed or turned. Kids these days are too clueless and far too willing to swallow that crap. What happened to the classics? Damn educational system. That's what happens when you cut the funding for schools, dumb kids who are easy prey for monsters. Next stop, communism.

Vampires are monsters. Forget everything you've seen in movies and on TV. Fuck Twilight, True Blood, and all those other things that portray them as beautiful creatures of darkness and sex. They're monsters, plain and simple. They exist on the lives and blood of living mortals. Vampires, in general, don't do a lot of that movie stuff. They're just obsessed with feeding. Those lucky enough to live for a century or more eventually move on to other things, but the younger vampires get hunted down and killed before their bloodlust becomes a serious threat to a population.

There is nothing posh or elegant about vampires, especially this one. For one, he reeked to the high hills. I could've probably tracked him by smell alone. I almost wished my nose didn't work. His stink was what you would get if you mixed a meth lab with a slaughterhouse. In addition to his saggy-seated, worn jeans and grubby undershirt, he was covered in dirt and grime as though he hadn't bathed even when he was human.

He pelted down the alleyway as fast as he thought he could go. Thank God young vampires are generally unaware of and have no clue how to control their new vampiric powers. Otherwise, he would've been leaving me in his dust. I'm fairly athletic due to my lifestyle and being of average height. I have long legs, allowing me to run good distances and cover a lot of ground. But I can't keep up with a supernatural predator that can outrun a car at city speed limits.

Newly minted vampires are like anyone else who is new to something. It's like learning a martial art. A student who has been studying for only a few weeks isn't going to know a lot or be much of a threat to anyone else. However, if they spend their whole lives learning and gaining experience, they can be extremely dangerous. It's the same with vampires. The longer a vampire is around, the more time they have to learn and grow in power, knowledge, and experience. So, the best time to take them out is when they are young and clueless.

This guy had only been one of the undead for about a week, but in that one week, he had single-handedly massacred everyone in his trailer park on the outskirts of Philadelphia. He had then turned it into his lair until I had been called in and smoked him out by setting the whole thing on fire. Vampires hate fire, especially being *on* fire. He'd fled in his rusted-out old truck, which turned into a spectacular chase with me hot on his tail.

He'd wrapped the pickup around two streetlights and a parked car. I pursued him as he fled down the alley, abandoning his truck. I kept my ax held low against my leg so no one would call the cops to report an ax-wielding maniac chasing people. I did *not* need the police to complicate my job even further. They didn't really warm to people with weapons, killing things that are hard to prove are not human, even when they are not a pile of ash.

He slipped in a puddle of something slimy in the street and went down to one knee as he tried to turn the corner down a branch of the alley, looking for a way back onto the street. He disappeared around the corner and from my sight as I slipped my hand into my jacket, going for my gun. If it looked like he could get away, I would've chanced taking a shot at him. I got lucky, and the alley he'd run into had a fifteen-foot chain link fence cutting off his escape. I drew my Colt 1911 as I came around the corner to find him attempting to climb the fence.

I aimed the .45 at the back of his skull and shouted. "Oi! Stinky! You might be a redneck if you're a smelly, undead bloodsucker."

Okay, it wasn't very witty, but give me a break. I had a long day, then spent most of the night burning down a trailer park and chasing a stupid country music reject across Philly. Philadelphia traffic isn't safe or sane at normal speed, even less so in the middle of a high-speed chase. So, my brain wasn't really in top form. The pieces of a great joke were in there somewhere. Just cross it out and write your own snarky joke.

It was enough to get his attention, and he turned from climbing the fence to face me. He snarled and bared his fangs. That would be enough to scare most people, but I'm a badass vampire slayer, and I've seen far scarier things. They usually wake me up screaming in the middle of the night.

His hands came up, looking more like bony claws than hands, into a position as if he was going to wave his arms and scream boo. Each finger was tipped with pointed blackening nails. They were sharp and strong enough to shred flesh and bone like paper or butter. I'd seen what he'd done to the woman who'd been his girlfriend and a couple other tenants of the park.

They weren't just gutted and torn apart. They'd been shredded so violently, their bodies and blood had been sprayed all over the place like a watermelon at a Gallagher show. It had been horrifying enough that I saw the horrifying mess every time I closed my eyes, and it pissed me off. That's the thing about vampires that gets to you: the level of violence they use on their victims. It's not the slow, sensual kiss-like bite on the neck that Bela Lugosi trademarked. It's bloody and violent when they feed. I've seen corpses nearly decapitated from deep bites and bones with marks where the fangs sheared through them.

"You asshole," it hissed. "Go fuck yourself!"

Blam!

I shot him in the face with the .45. The bullet hit him right above his right eye, leaving a dark hole and snapping his head back. Shooting a vampire doesn't kill them, nor does it really hurt them, but supernatural or not, they still have to deal with physics. A small projectile hitting you at about a thousand feet per second is still going to have the same impact, no matter what you are. The laws of physics are about the only thing I really have going for me since I'm just a plain old vanilla mortal. It's kind of unfair since I regularly go head-to-head with creatures that can bench-press a Buick.

The ACP rounds I use are a special soft-nosed variety designed for maximum impact, but not penetration. They hit like a runaway freight train, which is what you need to smack down something that can take getting hit by a train. The resulting impact knocked the hillbilly on his skinny ass. Like I said, physics makes fools of us all. I kept my pistol leveled at him as I closed the distance.

He recovered from being shot rather quickly, easy to do when you don't feel pain, and sprang to his feet. I fired again and again, putting round after round into its face, keeping it stunned and off balance while I moved in for the kill. Once the gun clicked empty, I didn't bother with care and ceremony. I just dropped the heavy gun. 1911 Colts are rugged and tough. They can take abuse and keep kicking. Timex watches could take a lesson from them. It hit the asphalt and bounced once before clattering across the ground. I shifted my grip to the ax in my right hand. With both hands on the heft, I stepped into the swing and aimed for the vamp's neck.

It was a beautiful swing. Probably the most perfect swing ever. Professional ballplayers like Barry Bonds would envy this swing. I aimed for the fences and let it fly. It should have taken his head clean off. It would've ended the fight right then and there. Yeah, yeah. Shoulda, coulda, woulda. But it didn't. It didn't because the bastard chose that exact moment to spontaneously tap into his vampire powers.

I don't know much about exactly how vampire powers work or how they manifest throughout a vampire's life. It's not really something anyone has really investigated. Mainly because they get killed, and there isn't much you can learn from them once you reduce them to a pile of ash. As they grow stronger, they gain control over their powers, and the powers themselves become stronger, but the exact science isn't really known.

You know how the human body can do superhuman feats, like a small woman lifting a car off her infant baby in dire situations? Apparently, that works for vampires and their powers, too. He bent at the knees, lowering himself just enough to lunge forward, and caught the blade of the ax between his teeth like some over-the-top action hero. Its fangs sank into the steel ax head like it was biting into butter, stopping my swing cold.

"Well...shit." I sighed.

I'm not a big guy, but I'm pretty strong, and as I said before, I know how to make the laws of physics work for me. A full power swing with a weighted instrument like that generates massive amounts of force and leverage. To stop it with just your teeth like that shows how super strong a vampire can be. As he stood, his mouth took the ax with it. I wrapped both arms around the handle and tried to pry it from the hick's nasty yellowed teeth, but I couldn't so much as budge it. I hung from the handle with all of my body weight, but I still couldn't dislodge it.

I saw the pure, malicious glint in its eyes just before it kicked me in the chest. Lucky for me, I had been hanging mid-air when I was kicked, so I absorbed most of the force easily, flinging my body through the air. Not so lucky when the kick sent me sailing backward into a solid brick wall. A human body plus a brick wall at velocity equals an ass load of pain. It's astounding how good I am at math equations when I'm in peril.

I never felt the impact of hitting the wall. There was only mind-numbing, earth-shattering pain. I slumped to the ground in a sitting position with my legs splayed out, propped up against the wall. The pain radiated out from my chest like wildfire. Three of my ribs, maybe four, must've been cracked, if not broken, for that level of agony. My chest clenched, causing me to cough up blood. It sprayed onto the ground and my coat. *Not good*. I hoped it was from biting my tongue on impact and not from something worse. Coughing up blood is usually a sign of internal bleeding.

My vision swam, and high-pitched whistles were sounding in my ears. Great, add a possible concussion to the list of injuries. I touched my ears. Good, no blood. That meant at least I didn't have a skull fracture. I cast my foggy mind about cataloging my body parts to see if anything else was broken or damaged. I was forgetting something, and it was important, but I couldn't remember what.

"Wakey, wakey. It's time for eggs and bakey," a country accent twanged from somewhere above me.

Oh yeah, the killer, white trash vampire who was about to tear me apart and make a rebel flag from my skin. Seriously, how whacked is it that the monster gets wittier snarks than the hero? So unfair, but if I live to tell the story later, I'll make sure to come up with a better line for myself. I will also make the redneck vampire two feet taller and add a few hundred pounds...and there were five of them.

I looked up at him. He was about my height, only a couple of inches short of six feet, but he was slimmer. He was slightly emaciated, not rail thin, but he definitely didn't get regular meals before he was infected. His ribs were prominent under his dirty wife-beater, and his hip bones stood out where his equally dirty jeans hung. He hadn't been wearing any shoes when he'd taken off. Had he not been a vampire, his cut-up feet would've pained him and been gushing blood. Infection alone would have been scary enough.

Ugh, tetanus.

He lowered his face to mine, and I was able to look into his burning eyes. The pupils had dilated until they were the size of half-dollars. Almost all the whites had disappeared. They were deep black voids that made me think of that old saying about looking into the abyss and how it looks back into you. They scared me, those eyes. They were devoid of human life, and whatever cold, evil entity had replaced their humanity was there naked and visible for the world to see, and for it to see the world. If he'd been around a hundred or so years older, I wouldn't have dared look into his eyes for fear of some form of mental attack or hypnosis. It was best to kill them before they learned those tricks.

The heady aroma of stale, decaying blood was on his breath. It poured out of his cavernous mouth and past the stalactite fangs. It was a real-life gateway to hell. The small, primal animal part of my brain that resides in the back of all human minds—a leftover from the days when we were further down the food chain—shrank and cowered from that mouth. We humans have not quite forgotten that fear of being eaten alive by a predator. We fool ourselves every day with our technology and civilization that we're beyond the animal kingdom of predator and prey. But we aren't, and we're still afraid of the things that go bump in the night.

"Hey, buddy, ain't killing a vampire hunter like a big deal for vampires?" he asked.

The question threw me off. I don't know if it was the concussion or that I was expecting some cliché bad guy line that new vampires seem to love spouting off, but I wasn't ready for it.

"Um, no, not really. We're just run-of-the-mill human beings. No real big to-do about killing us. Sorry." I leaned back a bit to get away from his killer bad breath, and slipped my hands into my pockets.

"Really? Ain't that a disappointment." He sighed, shifting his weight from foot to foot. His superpowers seemed to have dissipated now that he'd disarmed me. He held my ax in his left hand.

"Sorry about that. Hollywood tends to screw us all over. They never get it right," I answered. "So, are you still going to kill me?"

"Yup."

"Well, damn."

"Sorry, fella. But you burned down mah trailer, wrecked mah truck, shot me in the face, and tried to cut mah head off. It just wouldn't look right to just let ya go without sending a message." He rocked back on his heels and rubbed his fingers through the scruff on his chin.

"Well, in my defense, I didn't wreck your truck. That was you," I interjected. "And if it bothers you that much, just make it into a country song. Could be a hit."

"You think so?" he asked as if he was seriously contemplating it, and he probably was.

"No, and you're about the dumbest fucking undead white trash redneck that has ever whistled Dixie." I laughed and raised my legs, planting my boots in his chest.

His puzzled expression just made what came next all the sweeter.

Double *ka-blam*!

He was hit with a twin blast of fire and thunder that erupted from near the bottom of my boots as the rigs containing hidden shotguns under my pants legs tore into his chest. He was knocked flat on his back with two large burn patterns on the front of what was left of the undershirt. Beneath it was just chunks of red and pink meat shining with blood and mucus. He twitched and shuddered on the ground. Even a vampire can't shrug off having both lungs blown out with the force of a small truck.

His mistake was in letting me put my hands in my pockets. I have a nifty little setup. I took a pair of old single-shot 12-gauge shotguns, cut the barrels and stocks, then attached them to a set of old shin splints. They can be easily worn under loose-fitting pants, and my boots protect my feet from the resulting blast when fired. From there, all I have to do is unzip the special pockets I added to several pairs of pants, and slip my hands down to the triggers. Sneaky as hell, and uncomfortable at times, but it's a great ace in the hole when hunting vampires.

The rig is too bulky and illegal to wear all the time, so I regulate its use to planned hunts like tonight when I know it's going to get dangerous. Like I said, going up against preternatural monsters like vampires, I have to rely on luck and physics. I also think ahead and make sure to stack the deck as much as possible. There is no such thing as a fair fight or a dirty trick. Anything goes in a life-or-death fight.

I used the wall to push myself to my feet, still a little shaky. My chest screamed at me, those injured ribs making their existence known. Funny how you don't think about bones and other body parts until they're injured.

Once on my feet, I retrieved my ax from where the vampire had dropped it. The two holes left by the monster's fangs glared at me. There's nothing special about the ax. It's a plain old woodsman, thirty dollars at any Walmart, but I like to take care of my tools. The ax has a five-pound head on it with a hickory handle. It's sturdy and heavy, making it great for lopping off the heads of monsters in addition to cutting firewood. Another bonus is that the backside of the ax head can be used as a hammer to pound in stakes.

People have the wrong idea when it comes to killing vampires. Some think all you have to do is stake them through the heart, or you can use silver and garlic or whatever. It's all bunk. There are three steps for basic vampire killing: stake, sword, and fire.

Sounds simple, right? If only.

The first is what most people think of when you say vampire: the stake. But those people have the role of the stake wrong.

There is nothing special about it. Any good, dense wood will work, but anything strong and sharp will work, too, even if it's not wood. Unlike the Buffy TV show, just stabbing a vampire in the heart with a stake will not kill it, nor does it reduce it to dust. Vampires leave bodies. It's messy.

Stakes are merely there to pin the vampire down while you get to the head-cutting and fire part. You're probably getting sick of hearing it by now, but vampires, even with their supernatural powers, are still privy to the same snares of physics as everyone else. They can run fast and lift a ton, but they can't alter reality. Don't let anyone tell you any different because if they do, they probably hate you and are trying to get you killed.

Ideally, when you hunt vampires, you do it during the day when the sun is out. And they're asleep in their coffins. Though most vampires don't sleep in coffins. They can sleep anywhere they want, and I *do* mean *anywhere*. I'm not kidding. I once found one sleeping in a bathtub. Talk about your blood baths, pun. While the unsuspecting vampire slumbers, you have a chance to pound a stake through his chest. It doesn't have to be through the heart. Any part of the upper chest will work. The stake holds the vampire while you do the rest. Ever notice how hard it is to sit up when someone presses on the center of your chest or pins your shoulders? It's a whole center of gravity, symmetric thing.

Even a vamp can't do much when over two feet of wood is driven through their chest, forcing them off balance. That's not to say they can't get up or pull the stake out. I've had a couple of feisty ones. But honestly, staking is, in most cases, unnecessary. Skip step one and go directly to step two. Do not pass go. Do not collect two hundred dollars.

The sword, as it's called, is the act of cutting off a vampire's head. This is because the old vampire hunters of the Order used to use swords and large hunting knives to cut off their heads.

Severing a vampire's head doesn't kill them completely, and they can recover, given time to recuperate. It does disrupt their powers and makes it simpler to finish them off. I prefer to use an ax due to its weight and leverage, making it easier to behead the undead. Besides, no one uses swords anymore, and the ax is more practical than a bowie knife. That's still a step that can be skipped, it's just safer when they're powerless and headless.

Fire is the ultimate weapon against, well, anything. Fire is a purifying element. It burns away all and leaves behind nothing. It consumes good and evil alike, reducing everything back to a blank slate. Fire is man's greatest tool and weapon. It has allowed us to rise up against the darkness and claim this world as our own despite the dangers and monsters. Prometheus's gift to mankind can be used to either create or destroy.

Fire burns away at a vampire faster than they can regenerate. Eventually, there is nothing left of them. Vampire skin is also oddly flammable. I don't mean like if you fire off a spark near them, they go up like a Burmese monk at a protest. But once they're on fire, they have a hell of a time putting themselves out. If you got set on fire, you would do the old stop, drop, and roll. Ideally, it would smother the flames, and they would go out. On a vampire, the flames don't go out. Their skin seems to feed the flames and can even burn under water. I once watched a flaming vampire dive headfirst off the Ben Franklin Bridge and into the Delaware. A crowd of about twenty people joined me in watching him burn underwater for about half an hour. Someone even brought doughnuts. Good times.

Fire is the only sure way to kill a vampire. To be safe, you do all three to get the job done right. Stake them down, cut off the head, then set it all on fire and scatter the ashes to the wind. It's a horrible way to die, but so is being eaten alive.

I hefted the punctured ax to my shoulder and stood over the stunned vampire. His eyes grew wide in fear and understanding as he lay prostrate on the ground, his chest heaving as his obliterated lungs tried to perform their function. I guess his brain hadn't caught on yet that his body didn't need to breathe, so he could only struggle feebly. I raised the ax high and brought it down on his upturned throat. It cut through the undead monster's neck easily, severing its head and sending it rolling across the ally a few feet. The feet kicked violently once on impact, and the body lay still, but it wasn't dead. The eyes had gone dark, blank as though the evil inside them had gone. I knew better. It was still in there hiding, waiting, and biding its time. It would return if given that time.

I chopped off the arms and legs, and piled them on top of the body. Not really something you have to do, but I like to take extra precautions. I do *not* take chances with these things. Tossing the severed head on top of the pile, I fetched a can of gasoline from the trunk of my car. I doused the whole mess with the contents, and then touched a match to it. The fumes instantly exploded into flame, giving off blazing heat, light, and the god-awful smell of burning flesh.

I turned up my nose at the ghastly odor while I looked around for my dropped weapon. I found the Colt .45 lying half under a dumpster in a puddle of some unrecognizable goo. Wiping it off, I inspected it by the firelight for new nicks and scratches. It was old and beat up, but the rugged old 1911 still worked as if it had come off the factory line yesterday. It had belonged to my father, and his father before him.

I loaded a fresh mag into it and flicked the slide lock lever, chambering a new round. I clicked the safety on and holstered it under my jacket. I felt naked without the comforting weight of the weapon hanging in its shoulder holster. The pain in my ribs flared up again, and I lowered my hand from the holster to my side.

Ribs are some of the worst bones to break. They never really heal properly, and even when they do heal, they still hurt a little. I sat near the fire, trying to ignore the rank stench of barbecued vampire. I pulled up my shirt and inspected my ribs while the limbs made popping and crackling noises. I poked tenderly at them. *Woo*, good thing nothing was broken, just really tender and possibly cracked. I followed up the inspection by downing some aspirin to try to combat the epic league headache.

Human bodies take time to burn, and even then, it has to be particularly hot to reduce everything to fine ash. Crematoriums use blast furnaces. Thankfully, vampire bodies burn more intensely and hotter than human ones. So, it saves hunters from having to cart them off to places equipped for such things. Even then, I had to hang around for a while, and the wee hours of the morning turned into the late hours of the morning. I got to sit back and watch the sun come up over the city skyline as the corpse turned to ash and the flames died.

In the end, all that was left was a pile of powdery white ashes. I scooped as much of it as I could into a large Ziploc bag. It's amazing how small the remains of a body can be once you burn away all the excess. You can be as big and strong as you want, but if, at the end of the day, you end up in a plastic sandwich bag, you know you've been thoroughly trounced.

I took some slightly childish pleasure in being the winner. Hey, the asshole had nearly managed to beat my ass with one kick. I take my victories where I can.

Chapter 2

I drove my old 1975 Plymouth Road Runner to my office. Okay, that's a bit of a lie. I *tried* to drive to the office. In reality, I spent nearly an hour sitting in morning rush hour with a bag of vamp ashes on the passenger seat. I hate doing that because it kind of looks like I'm driving around with a kilo of drugs sitting next to me. It's not an exaggeration, either. I was pulled over once, and the cop got the wildest idea I really was driving around with a bag of cocaine. I don't know why. It's not like I'm an insufferable smartass who makes wiseacre comments that annoy people. Okay, maybe I am, but I blame the cop for not having a sense of humor and taking sarcasm too seriously.

Driving a classic muscle car would make most people happy with having to sit in traffic where other people can see their cool car and be envious. Not for me. I live on a budget. While the Road Runner can haul ass with the best of them, it's not the prettiest girl at the dance. It looks like a rusty piece of crap, and I'm constantly getting pulled over because the car doesn't look street legal. I'm not talking about the hot-rodder kind of street legal. I'm talking safety-hazard kind of street legal. The car's body is mostly a nasty primer gray with large areas of rust and some holes in the fenders near the wheel wells. There are dents everywhere, and a couple of serious ones in the hood, grill, and bumper on the passenger's side with a matching spiderweb pattern of cracked glass in the windshield.

They were left over from a particularly hard-to-kill vampire. It was a lot easier once I'd nailed him head-on with the car and pinned him to a roadside barrier. The Road Runner is a tough old bird. Its steel body makes it nearly invincible, plus I like it. I think of us as kindred spirits. I like to see myself as the Road Runner. Outwitting poor old Wile E. Coyote, and always staying one step ahead of danger. Though, in actuality, I probably have more in common with Wile E. and falling off cliffs when my plans backfire.

Did I mention there's no air conditioner in the car? Or that my windows don't roll down? Or that we were experiencing an unusually hot Indian summer, and even at nine in the morning, it got hot enough to roast a turkey in there?

Rush hour is even more unbearable when you spend it inside a rolling sweat lodge. I had killed two bottles of water and was getting sorely tempted to pull out my gun to shoot air holes in the roof.

I finally arrived at my office on Margaret Street. It was a three-floor walkup, and guess which floor my office is on. Yep, the third floor. Ever walk up two flights of stairs with cracked ribs? Not pleasant. By the time I reached the front door of my outer office, I was wheezing and doubled over in pain. I leaned against the wall opposite the door with its sign in big black letters on the glass.

T. Halson: Vampire Hunter, it read. It looked like one of those old private eye doors from a 1940 noir movie. I liked it.

While the door and my business cards say vampire hunter, my business license is actually for pest extermination. I'm licensed by the city to hunt and kill vampires.

Okay, City Hall thinks I'm trapping raccoons and spraying for silverfish. What they don't know can't hurt them. Despite that, I do run a legitimate business. I pay taxes and everything. While I don't make a lot, I will never be rich, I do manage to not only pay my rent, but I can afford a secretary. So, I eat ramen and canned soup most nights, but it's worth it to not have to do my own scheduling and filing.

My actual office is made of two rooms on the top floor of a converted three-story house. The first room is big enough for several filing cabinets, a desk, and a small waiting area consisting of a handful of cheap folding chairs with Mort's Funeral Home across their backs. This is the room most people see. They don't get further than my secretary Anita's desk. She serves as my junkyard dog.

Anita is a large Black woman who grew up in the projects and doesn't take shit from anyone, even me. She raised an eyebrow when I dragged myself through the door. Battered, bruised, sleep-deprived, and covered in sweat and gore. Anita gave me the look of a mother who was tired of, but not surprised by, a rowdy kid tracking mud into her clean kitchen.

"You're late, boss. It sets a bad example for your employees when you drag your sorry ass in an hour after opening and making everyone wait on you."

"I was working all night, and never got a chance to go home. Yet, here I am to do it all over again. So technically, I am setting a good example of hard work ethic, and you're the one being lazy."

"Boy, I don't have no problem with smacking you upside the head, boss or not." Anita has only about twenty years on me, but still treats me like a kid.

"You do, and you're fired," I responded with a serious look on my face.

"Fire me, and you'll be out of a job. I don't see your lazy ass sitting here answering phones, making appointments, and filing papers. Heck, I should fire you." She rolled her eyes and made a little exasperated gesture with her hands.

"Hey now, don't forget I'm the one who signs your paycheck."

"Honey, you don't sign nothing. If I didn't sign your name to everything, we'd both be out of a job." She shifted some papers around on her desk and handed me several small yellow sticky notes.

"Yeah, well, as long as you don't use it for evil." I took the notes and glanced at them.

The two top ones were appointment times for meeting clients later this afternoon. Good, that meant I could take a nap until then. The third was a notice to call Captain Bullard of the Philadelphia PD. Oh, goodie, the police wanted an update on how the vampire hunt turned out last night.

"Thanks, Anita." I dropped the bag of vampire ash onto her desk, and she recoiled from it. "Toss that into the bin and let Bullard know his little trailer park problem has been taken care of, and make sure they put the check in the mail."

Philly PD's contracting jobs pay a lot of my bills. Though, my services go on the city records as precinct building fumigation or infestation assessment. Neat, huh? Apparently, the guys at City Hall don't want it to be known they pay a vampire hunter.

"Is that our country boy?" She gingerly lifted the bag with two fingers, keeping it far away from her body.

"What's left of him."

She dropped the bag into the bottom drawer of one of the file cabinets and kicked it shut. Her reaction to the undead amused me. She has a lot of personality, which brightens my mostly dreary day-to-day job. She's bright, loud, and dresses like a grandmother, who happens to be a retired hooker. Lots of tight-fitting clothing and low-hanging lines, making her large figure look like someone tried to stuff sausage into a wrapper two sizes too small.

Her hair was sunset red, matching her long nails, and piled on top of her head in a sort of beehive/bun hybrid style. She wore an animal print top with a sequin skirt and red high heels that matched. I had no clue what she weighed, but she was a hefty woman with a large personality to match. A lot of woman, and it makes her an excellent deterrent to keep people from just barging in on my inner office. God help the poor S.O.B. who tries to get around her.

"I'm worn out and need some sleep, so hold all my calls."

Anita snorted. We were not a hotbed of activity.

"And if anyone comes in looking for me, I'm not here, and won't be back 'til after lunch."

"You're the boss. At least, until some big nasty vamp tears your head off."

"Nah, never gonna happen. I'm too good and way too lucky for that." I smiled.

"Yeah, yeah, you're really tough when it's daylight out."

"Yep, total badass," I agreed.

"Well, Mister Badass, lay down before you fall over." She smiled as I opened the door to my inner sanctum.

My inner sanctum is just a single room, about ten-by-ten feet. It's hardly bigger than a closet, and looks like a cross between a messy accountant's office and someone's old tool shed. In the center of the room was my desk. It's not big, but it holds a surprising amount of paperwork and clutter. Behind the desk is a large map of the city with push pins and string forming a psychotic spiderweb of connections meaningless to anyone but me, and some of them, not even to me.

On one side of the room are a couple more file cabinets stuffed with badly filed paperwork, topped with a coffee can of rusty iron nails and an old crossbow. It's a really old medieval-style one and heavy as hell, but it takes forever to draw the bowstring back and load a bolt into it. Great for staking vampires, but impractical, and I didn't have any bolts for it. Across from the cabinets was a workbench covered with more papers and tools.

I closed the door and clicked on the one naked bulb that hung from the ceiling.

There are no windows in my inner office. Not that I don't like sunlight. It's just harder to fall asleep at my desk with bright light pouring through. I took off my coat and tossed it over the back of my desk chair. It was a heavy canvas coat, and I'm not sure whether it's called a trench coat or a duster, but it's long, dark brown, and stops just below my knees. Long coats are great for concealing weapons and tools, plus they have lots of pockets for sticking other stuff. I removed the shoulder holster I carried my gun in and hung it from the hook on the back of the door. The gun itself went into the desk drawer. Under the coat and holster, I wore a white button-up collared dress shirt with the sleeves rolled up to my forearms. There were spots on the shirt from where I had coughed up blood on it. Luckily, it was from a bite on the inside of my mouth, the result of the impact against the wall.

I reached up my sleeves and removed a pair of small knives in sheaths that had been strapped to my upper arms and put them on the workbench. I took another knife in its sheath from my belt at the small of my back and tossed it onto the workbench, too. I also removed two small plastic sport bottles with squeeze tops containing holy water. That was followed by removing my nylon belt. The belt had a trick buckle that was a hidden knife. I can't sleep while wearing a belt. It's uncomfortable. It was added to the pile of knives, along with a straight razor I keep in my boot.

Sitting on the desk, I rolled up my pant legs and kicked off my boots so I could remove the gun rigs on my legs. They saved my life last night, and I was glad I had them. I popped each shotgun open in turn, ejecting the spent shell, and loaded fresh ones into them. I snapped them closed, and onto the workbench they went. I have a sawed-off pump action Remington I keep in my trunk for hunting when I don't use the rig. The problem is, it's hard to use a shotgun and carry an ax at the same time.

I had left the ax in the car. There was no need for it since it was damaged. I would have to pick up a new one later. Easy come, easy go. As I said, they're cheap and available at any hardware store. So, it's not like it's especially hard to come by axes. I would have to add it to my list of items to pick up on my way home. Milk, eggs, new ax, bullets, holy water, peanut butter—you get the idea.

I swept all the papers and clutter off the desk and onto the floor. It's okay. I would clean up the mess later. Okay, okay, I wouldn't clean it up. I'd leave it for Anita to do. It would give her something besides the filing, scheduling, and everything else she does around the place. I wouldn't want to make her feel unneeded.

I rolled onto the now clear desk, taking care not to do anything to cause my ribs to remind me of their injuries. Laying on my back on the desk like that, my legs stuck off and hung down at the knee. I turned onto my side and curled up into a fetal position. Pulling my coat over me like a blanket, I closed my eyes and finally fell asleep.

Chapter 3

It was dark, and I was in pain. My back had been ripped wide open, exposing the muscle and bones of my spine. The agony was unbearable, but I couldn't pass out. The screams kept the blackness of unconsciousness at bay. They were dying, and I couldn't do anything to help them. Fangs, as long as sabers, dripped endless rivers of scarlet blood. The screams...the screams bored into my skull like a power drill. I could feel them all the way down my mutilated back.

I desperately tried to move. Stretching out my arms as far as I could, I dug my nails into the hardwood flooring and tried to drag myself forward. The effort caused the nerves in my back to explode in protest. I had no sensation below my waist, making my legs useless. The pain sapped all my strength, and it doubled every time I tried to move, making my arms limp noodles.

I could do nothing except drown in my helplessness while they died. It was eating them, and slowly. One of the worst ways to go, and there was nothing I could do. I was just so useless.

I was too weak to defend myself, much less anyone else. Hot, bitter tears of anger blurred my vision as rage welled up inside me. It grew and built like a burning inferno. I tried to focus that hate on something I could use to get my broken body up and moving.

The vampire, a prehistoric-looking creature from Hell, was tearing apart people I cared about. It turned its monstrous attention to where I lay. It seemed impossibly huge as it towered over me. Its long arms and dinosaur-like talons reached for me.

A scream rose in my throat, but I couldn't let it out. I was too scared. Those hands wrapped around me, drawing me towards the abyss of its mouth. Its hands froze my skin where it touched me—the cold touch of death's embrace.

It lowered its head to my neck, and its giant fangs bit into my throat. My hot blood sprayed out in jets. It gushed over my shoulder and down my chest. Its teeth bit deeper as its tongue lapped up my warmth. My bones crunched, and the sounds of them echoed in my ears.

The screams came.

They strangely sounded like rings. Kind of like the rings of a telephone. More specifically, my telephone.

I nearly fell off my desk as I groggily flailed about trying to find it. It wasn't on the desk where it was supposed to be. It was on the floor.

My chest hurt, and a ghost memory of pain ran down the scar on my back. That was usually an omen of bad things to come. *Oh, goodie.*

Most people would be super pissed off about being woken up from some awesome sex dream about Olivia Wilde. Even though I was still dead tired, my limbs were lead weights. My head felt like fat Octoberfest beer wenches in spiked clogs were dancing in it, and my rib cage hurt so bad, my lungs were being squeezed by a python. I was glad to be pulled out of that hellish nightmare.

Scrambling around, tossing papers right and left, I looked for the phone. It had been on my desk with the papers until I'd tossed them onto the floor so I could sleep. It was surprising the handset managed to stay in the cradle. Yeah, I have an old-fashioned handset phone circa the 1980s. It doesn't have a rotary dial, but it does still have cords. Don't get the wrong idea. I'm just too cheap to spring for a new one. What? It still works, and it's heavy, just in case I need to hit someone with it. Also, I can just leave it off the hook to avoid calls.

I managed to find the cord and followed it until it led me to the jack in the wall. I promptly turned around and followed it in the other direction until I found the ringing phone and put it to my ear.

"Tobias Halson, Vampire Hunter. Fuck off," I said groggily into the mouthpiece.

"I admire your commitment to creative advertising, Halson, but I would think telling prospective customers to fuck off might hurt your sell." The baritone voice of Detective Bullard spoke from the earpiece. "You also might want to try calling the police back when they leave several notices with that ball-busting howitzer of a woman you call a secretary, especially if you expect to get paid after burning down half the city."

"It wasn't half the city, just one trailer park. Oh, yeah, and a tiny bonfire in an alley over on Prestborne." I rubbed the back of my hand across my eyes.

"God damn it, Halson. It's getting harder to justify to the powers that be about keeping you on as a consultant when you're running around setting fires, blowing up buildings, carrying illegal weapons, and skinning God knows what on public sidewalks."

"That only happened once," I interjected.

"The point is, I have enough people to deal with who think you're more of a problem than these monsters, and most of them want me to lock *you* up," Bullard finished angrily.

"Look, I'm tired and in pain, and unless you're calling for something other than to check up on your toasted neck biter, who is now just a bag of ashes sitting in my file cabinet, thank you very much, kiss my ass, Bullard, because I care less about your internal politics than you do." The stress and weariness put more of an edge in my tone than I meant to, but I'd been working with Detective Darren Bullard for over a year now. Bullard had been a cop for well over twenty years, and knew how to read between the lines and work with uncooperative assholes.

"Unfortunately, this is another matter, but I will pass on the word we have another Mr. Crispy ready for pick up. Bring it with you, and you can drop it off here at the scene." Bullard completely ignored my rant and changed the subject.

"What scene, and why the hell would I want to come down there?" Sleep was still muddling my brain, and the headache wasn't helping.

"After spending all night with the fire crew overseeing the attempt to control the chaos you unleashed, I got a call before I could go home to my wife's hot cooked breakfast that we had another one of those cases in Center City. I need you down here to confirm it's an official PSIC case."

Bullard was in charge of Philadelphia's Special Investigation Case department. On paper, they're the guys who take the weird or difficult-to-explain cases and make sure everything wraps up neatly with a bow. In reality, it's the department where they shelve the losers and political rivals. If you screw up or scare a higher-up into thinking you could be a threat to their job, you get stuck in the PSIC unit.

Another feature that distinguishes the PSIC unit was they're the ones who have to deal with supernatural cases. If there is a body found drained of blood or turned inside out, PSIC is brought in to find out what did it since no other department wants to deal with a headache or be seen as crazy when they go on about vampires and monsters. That's why the other departments and cops insult them by referring to them as the Psych unit. I'm not sure if it's Psych as in Psychotic or Psych as in a joke. I just know it's not a compliment.

However, six years ago, Bullard was put in charge of PSIC, and he turned it into a respectable department, and was able to explain every single weird case as something boring and mundane. Then, a year after hiring the city's best and only hunter, they were able to not only explain, but actually close most of their cases.

Though Bullard has the stones to take his assignment and shove it in the faces of his superiors with how well he does it, he—and, by extension, the entire Philly Police Department and Mayor's office—don't really want people to know they contract some dangerous possible whack job to run around and exterminate things that go bump in the night. So, instead, I bill them under the guise of pest extermination. Philly's police precincts have shot up immensely among the national standings as some of the most infested in the US.

You see, people don't want to admit supernatural stuff exists. They walk side-by-side with it every day, but they pretend it's not there. They do it because they don't want it to be real, they don't know how to defend against it, and it makes them feel helpless and afraid. It's easier for them to just ignore it and chalk it up to things they *can* explain or understand.

Man's fear motivates a lot of his darker aspects, especially ignorance. I understand it because I feel the same way about magical stuff.

I'm a monster guy. If a vampire kills a sorority dorm full of co-eds, I'm called in to track it down and turn it to ash. The PSIC calls me in because some new bad nasty is causing trouble, and I sally forth to slay it. On the other hand, if some inconsiderate dope is playing with some spell-heavy McGuffin, they are gonna have to crack open the Yellow Pages and find someone else. I don't do magic because I don't know how to defend against it. I'm pretty much all physical, and have no way to deal with pure energy and whatever else magic is made of. Probably pixie dust and unicorn farts. People hate feeling helpless in the face of something more powerful than them. It goes back to that primal, not-forgotten part of our reptile brain.

"What makes you think it's something from my side of the street?" I asked.

"This is one of those things you have to see for yourself. I can't discuss it over the phone now, but I need you down here before the coroner and the CSI guys can haul off the body."

He finished by giving me the address of a swanky business complex plaza in Center City.

I whistled as I wrote it down on a piece of paper and stuffed it into my pocket. After that, I hung up on Bullard. I always hang up first, and checked the address with my map. I looked at the time and groaned. It was just past noon. A trip to Center City with no AC on a hot day during lunch hour was going to be hell.

Chapter 4

I arrived at the crime scene almost an hour later. The area was roped off with bright yellow police tape. One of the uniforms gave me a skeptical look as I pulled up in the Road Runner. It must have been hotter than holy hell standing out in the sun and heat wearing his street blues. He was easily a few dozen pounds overweight with a gut that threatened to fall down over his duty belt. Despite the dark color of his uniform, I could make out damp patches under his arms. Sweat ran down his brow from his cap and into his piggy little eyes. He kept his eyes on me as I got out of the car and approached the police line. I didn't blame him. I looked like a cross between a vagrant and an axe murderer. I gave him my most charming smile as he gave me a once over.

I had thrown my coat back on after getting out of the car. Not a lot of people wear long coats like mine, especially on hot days. I needed it to cover my gun and other equipment I carried. My shaggy hair was disheveled and damp with sweat. I had at least a day's worth of stubble growth, and my under eyes were dark from lack of sleep, looking like two burnt holes in a blanket. All of which stood out in more contrast, thanks to my pale skin. I don't get a lot of sun since I spend most of my days asleep or hiding in my windowless office.

"Hold it right there, buddy! This is a crime scene. You see that police tape? It means beat it." He held one hand to my chest. Not touching me, just showing me I wasn't to go any further.

I hate it when people do things like that. It's the same action that makes me say wisecracks. I resisted the urge to spout something stupid and antagonize him. I showed him my laminated consultant card, issued to me by the police department.

He glared at it as though it had insulted his mother. He compared the picture on the photo ID to me. I hate taking pictures for IDs and licenses. I always end up looking like a terrorist or something, and I don't photograph well.

He turned and said something into his radio I couldn't quite hear, checking to make sure my ID was legit and I wasn't some reporter trying to con my way into a crime scene. Reporters are a pain in the ass, especially if they catch wind that it's a PSIC case. The less you want to say about something, the more interested the press is in it. Tell them everything about the most brutal killing spree in the world, and they don't care. Refuse to tell them anything about the mugging of an old lady, and they are pulling a Watergate in your office to uncover the conspiracy of the ages.

He gave me a sour frown like he wasn't happy he didn't get to bash my head in, and handed me back my card. He lifted the police tape to allow me past.

I tried to keep from saying something that would make things worse, I really did. I looked over my shoulder at him and smiled.

"Have a nice day, officer," I said sweetly. I have no idea why people don't like me.

I made my way through the throngs of cops and CIS person-nel. Real crime scenes are nothing like the ones on TV. For one, on TV, everyone is well-dressed, bright-eyed, and quick with some witty joke. Here, everyone looked like they were holdovers from the night shift. They were bleary-eyed with mussed hair and badly wrinkled clothing. At least I wasn't the worst-looking guy here. Heck, some of the cops made me look downright well-groomed.

Their moods weren't much better, either. It looked like there were half a dozen yelling matches on the sidewalk as a result of overworked men with strained nerves, and the heat of the day was only going to make it worse. Another thing they miss on those TV shows is the sense of urgency you feel on a real scene. Everyone is in a hurry, trying to do their jobs as quickly as possible or impatiently waiting for someone else to finish so they can get to it.

The place was a powder keg, just waiting for a spark to set it all off. Probably not the best place for a guy with all the charm and grace of a blunt buzz saw, making these situations the equivalent of the Human Torch farting in a Chinese fireworks factory. I really needed to watch my step in this minefield.

Then, a pretty young woman with long blonde hair pulled back in a ponytail stepped in front of me.

Oops, too late. *Boom*, the Vietnam War is over, and everyone is dead. Thanks for playing, folks.

Detective Alex Benson wore a short black t-shirt and a pair of skintight jeans that looked like she'd been poured into them. The shirt fluttered in a gust of random wind, showing off a nice patch of her firm stomach. Her sweat-covered skin held hints of toned muscle beneath, causing parts of me to become equally firm.

I tried to think about dead puppies and forced a smile. Ben-son and I do not get along well despite our relative ages and backgrounds. It had something to do with the fact that, during our first meeting, I may or may not have mistaken her for a secretary, and I may have slapped her on the ass. I don't remember too well because she threw me out a second-floor window seconds later, where I landed on a fire escape, and everything was fuzzy from the concussion.

She won't admit it, but she totally has the hots for me.

She has beautiful, bright blue eyes that sparkled playfully in the hot afternoon light. They were that shocking, nearly inhuman blue found in magazine models and on TV commercials. They were so like, yet unlike my cold, empty ones. Even though she'd been a cop since long before I'd known her, all the death and evil hadn't managed to taint her yet. Leaving her pure, but not naïve. She knew the world wasn't fair and walked with a chip on her shoulder.

Benson was a Nordic goddess, all hard planes and liberal curves in all the right places. Me, I'm built more along the lines of a heavy stick used to whack stupid people with. Her well-toned body and muscle definition were the result of hours of hard work in the gym. In contrast to mine, which was the result of regularly missed meals. I'm almost certain I would've been taller had my diet been steadier, or maybe not.

If Alex was a goddess and I was a blunt stick, then Detective Darren Bullard was a Sherman tank. He loomed above her head as he appeared behind her and put his hand on her shoulder. He was more than a head taller than her and was nearly three or four times wider. Bullard was a beast. He stood a little over six and a half feet tall, and had to weigh close to three hundred pounds, to which every ounce was muscle.

He needed all that size and muscle to combat the things that lurked in the darkness. It also helped him to keep Alex from tearing my skull out and repurposing it as a coffee mug. The hand-on-the-shoulder trick was how Bullard reinforced his authority among the police under his command. Every single one of them knew when one of those big paws was placed on your shoulder, you kept your mouth shut and did just what the boss man told you to.

Being that I was an outside contractor, and Bullard had seen me in all my glory doing the job the very first second we'd met, which sort of entailed saving his life, I was exempt from his "charms." That, and the fact I flaunt authority figures on reflex and principle. I have issues. Bullard was a passable double for Michael Clark Duncan from that Stephen King movie. I don't know where he got his suits, but if they had charged him by the yard, they were making a killing.

"Good, you're here. Let's get this freak show on the road." His voice was like a low-hanging thundercloud, deep and rolling.

I gave Alex a big shit-eating grin, showing her every single one of my teeth. I could almost see the smoke curl out of her ears, knowing she wanted very badly to say something witty or chiding, but couldn't.

Bullard and Benson led me through the throng to the center of the activity. The crowd thinned out, and I could see what Bullard had called me down here for. It was a dead body, twisted and mangled. The arms, legs, and neck were twisted at odd angles human bodies were not meant to bend. Just the sight of broken bones made my aches and pains howl, a reminder that not twelve hours ago, my own body had gone through a similarly brutal beating. There were shards of glass all around and under the body. There were even several shards stuck *into* the body itself.

"See anything odd?" Bullard asked as he watched me study the scene.

I looked at the body, the glass, and then up at the office building in whose shadow we were standing. I didn't see any broken windows from where I was. That meant if the glass came from a broken window, it was up farther than could be seen from our spot on the ground. Craning my neck back that far to look up caused a lightning bolt of pain to shoot through my skull. Great, possible whiplash on top of the rest of the catalog of injuries I had racked up.

"There's no blood," I said. "A fall from any height, lethal or not, and there would be blood all over the place. But, guessing from the number of injuries and how bad they are, he fell from a long, long way up. Meaning when he hit, he should've splattered like a water balloon full of blood. Yet, all his damage is from the impact and glass. Since there's no blood, you're thinking a vampire sucked him dry, then chucked him out the window."

"That, and these marks." Alex turned the man's head, and as she spoke, she showed me the right side of the man's neck. "Vampire bite marks."

Sure enough, there were two dark puncture wounds on the side of the man's neck. I leaned over to get a closer look.

"That's weird," I answered. "But those are not bite marks."

She gave me a questioning *don't bullshit me* glare. "Then what are they?"

"Not sure. They look like large gauge needle marks. When a vampire bites, it tears the throat out like an animal attack. This looks like a movie version of a vampire bite, something you'd see in an old black-and-white double feature. Anyone who's seen a real vampire bite knows that. This looks more like some amateur trying to make it look like a vampire attack." I stood, my lower back popping with the sound of a small caliber handgun going off.

"I knew the minute I saw it," Bullard broke in. "But see that fancy glass all around us? It's specialized safety glass. They make it for high-rises like this. The windows don't open, and the glass is tempered safety like they make for cars, but much stronger to keep people from having accidents or suicides by throwing themselves through a window. That's why jumpers do it from the roof or a balcony. It's hard as hell to break one of those windows, so it would take something really strong to throw someone through one."

"Yeah, yeah. I saw that Will Smith movie, too, Bullard. I know about safety glass, but that doesn't mean this is supernatural, just really, really weird." I rocked back on my heels, contemplating the information in front of me. "What floor was he tossed from?"

"He's Donald Baker, one of the top executives," Alex answered me. "His office was on the top floor. Whatever it was tossed his body through the window, and it fell over thirty stories."

"Have you talked to the other executives, security, the building owners? Etcetera."

"We have officers interviewing everyone," Bullard said. "Based on what evidence we have on hand, we're proceeding as if this is an official PSIC case. I want you to look around and see if you can't find something that proves one way or another that this is or isn't a vampire, or some other nasty. You'll get your normal retainer and your pay per hour through the department until it's solved either way."

"Oh well, if you're going put it so sweetly... Bullard, you know I'm not an investigator. I'm an exterminator. You find them, I kill them. If I have to find them, too, then why do I need you guys?" I joked.

"We're the ones you bill, and the city pays that bill." Bullard mopped the sweat from his bald head. "And your card says *Vampire Hunter*, so get hunting."

"Fine, fine. Are they gonna be okay with me stalking around, doing my bloodhound thing?" I looked towards the office entrance where several nebbish office worker types stood gawking or being questioned by uniformed cops. They wore suits, ties, and glasses. Not exactly the kind of atmosphere I would blend into.

"If they don't, we can charge them with obstruction of justice and interference with a police investigation," Alex chimed in with a note of contempt in her voice.

"Wow, babe, ever hear the expression *bull in a China shop*? Subtlety, that's what you are, the very definition. No wonder you became a regular Sherlock Holmes."

"Shut up, asshole. At least I don't dress like a low-budget *Matrix* extra."

"Hey now, this coat is a staple of the office. Like your badge, only sexier." I gave her my shit-eating grin again.

"Now, kids, if you keep bickering, I'm going have to give you two corner time," Bullard interrupted us, trying to head off another altercation caused by conflicting egos.

Benson stuck her tongue out at me.

It was totally childish, so I stuck my tongue out at her and upgraded it by wiggling my fingers on either side of my head.

She responded by rolling her eyes.

"You're so immature." She turned to the EMTs to tell them they could remove the body.

This action caused both of the detectives to become distracted, so I seized the moment. Quickly checking to make sure no one else was watching, I stooped, snatched up a jagged piece of the glass, and shoved it into my coat pocket as fast as I could. Just as my hand had slipped into my pocket, Bullard and Benson turned back to face me. My face instantly heated like a kid who'd just gotten caught with his hand in the cookie jar.

They both gave me questioning looks. Damn detectives, they notice everything.

"What the hell are you up to?" Alex probed.

"I gotta pee," I blurted. Damn, I suck at spur-of-the-moment quips. I usually think up my snarky replies ahead of time. "So, yeah, got to go."

I turned and started marching towards the building entrance and away from the crime scene.

"You're such a child, Halson," she called after me.

I didn't look back at her. I just raised one hand and gave her one of those dismissive offhand waves as I walked away.

Chapter 5

I made my way to the front entrance of the office building. I passed several employees being questioned by the police. No one paid me any mind as I slipped by and pushed through the revolving glass doors into the lobby. My coattails got caught in the door as it turned, causing me to stumble a bit and killing my cool factor. I liked to think I looked all awesome and Hollywood when I entered a place with my long dark coat swirling around me, giving me an air of mystery and danger. Nearly pulling a faceplant in the entranceway did nothing to inspire awe or amazement in people.

I caught myself before I could completely fall over and embarrass myself entirely. I quickly righted myself and found every single pair of eyes in the room on me. My cheeks heated. I kept a straight face and strode to the pretty young woman at the reception desk. She was cute, but her expression marred her beauty. She scowled at me, obviously not used to awkward, disheveled men stumbling into the building. She looked like a teenager dressed up in a librarian costume. She had her sleek dark hair pulled back into a tight bun, adding to her strait-laced ensemble. Her eyes glared at me from behind horn-rimmed glasses. They were old-fashioned and out of place on her.

I suddenly felt really out of place myself and underdressed standing here. I pondered what her reaction would've been had she known that under my coat was an array of weapons. I envied people like her, who were ignorant and unaware of the danger all around them. I sometimes wondered what it would be like to have a normal life. You know, one without all the blood and death.

I gave her my biggest and warmest smile, then asked her where the elevators were and what floor Donald Baker's office was on. She gave me a suspicious look until I flashed my laminated consultant card at her and told her I was with the police. She pointed me towards the rear of the entrance space to a set of metallic elevators that gleamed in the afternoon sunlight. I gave her another smile and thanked her. Which did nothing to thaw her coldness towards me.

I left her to glare at my back, and I shuffled off to the elevators. I fingered the shard of glass in my pocket as I jabbed my thumb at the Up button. It was hard and smooth, cool to my touch. My fingers slid along the plane of the glass until it reached the jagged edge. I ran the pad of my index finger along the ridge where it had broken. It was rough and oddly uniform for broken glass.

The doors finally slid open, and people filed out. None of them looked at me. They kept their gazes down and focused on nothing. People in big cities develop a natural ability to not see anything around them. It's a survival instinct to help them survive. Sort of the "if I can't see it, it can't hurt me" school of thought. People sleep easier if they can ignore all the unpleasant things that go bump in the night. People go above and beyond to ignore the monsters. It's easier for everyone that way.

I was the first to step onto the elevator, turned around, and put up a hand to stop the other people from getting on with me.

"Sorry folks, police business," I said as one especially displeased balding man gave me the stink eye over his paper.

I reached over and pressed the Close button while holding down the floor number of Baker's office until the doors shut and the lift started moving. This was an old police and fireman's trick that locked the elevator so it wouldn't stop on any other floor until it reached the one selected. This meant I wouldn't be interrupted by anyone until I reached my floor. I slumped against the rear wall and pulled the shard of glass from my pocket. It was about five to six inches long and almost teardrop-shaped. I turned the shard so I could examine the cross-section, held it up to the light, and squinted. A thin, almost invisible black line ran the length of the cross-section.

What I know of safety glass comes from cars. Car windshields are made up of two panes of glass held together by a plastic adhesive sheet. The purpose of the plastic sheet is to hold glass together when damaged to prevent large shards from flying off and causing further injuries. Well, that was the theory, anyway. I'm not sure how well it works in practice. The important thing is that the plastic liner typically used is clear, but this one looked to be black. I turned the shard back over to the smooth side and held it up to the light, looking through it. There was no hint of any tinting to the glass. I frowned at the fragment, then put it back in my pocket as the lift chimed and the doors slid open.

Baker's office was on the top floor as part of some corporate offices for the top executives. I stepped off the elevator into the extravagantly appointed reception hall. The room was furnished with several comfy-looking chairs and a rather simplistic coffee table set with high-class magazines like Forbes and GQ. There were plants placed around the offices that were too perfect to be anything other than fake.

Directly across from the elevators, about twenty feet away, was a large desk in front of a sort of buffer wall. The kind of thing built not to create a real barrier, but to block sound or line of sight, and to let visitors know they're not worthy of gazing upon the superior beings who worked beyond. The woman sitting at that desk looked like the older and meaner big sister of the one in the lobby. She had the same tight dark bun hairstyle and horn-rimmed glasses. Even her pinstripe suit was nearly identical.

She gave me the same disapproving expression as the lobby girl, though hers looked slightly bored, as if she'd been scowling at lesser mortals all day. With all the cops and CSI personnel who'd been going in and out, she probably had.

I gave her my patented smile. My face was beginning to hurt from all the overuse today, but she wasn't impressed.

"Do you have an appointment?" she asked.

"I'm with the police, ma'am." I flashed my ID card at her. "Can you tell me where Mr. Baker's office is?"

She looked me up and down, and made me feel even shabbier than usual with her designer suit and executive reception area. Like a little kid who'd been rolling around in the mud and was now being scolded by a prim schoolteacher.

"The police have already left, sir," she said coldly. "They shut down the office for most of the day with their crime scene nonsense."

I was thrown a bit by her lack of concern for the fact that one of her bosses had just gotten exsanguinated and thrown out a window. It's one thing to hear about how indifferent people can be to others, but seeing that kind of coldness for yourself is a completely different thing.

"They said they'd finished about an hour ago, and left for the day, so unless you have a warrant or an appointment, I cannot help you, sir."

She put an inflection on the word *sir* as if she meant it as an insult rather than a title. I hate when people look down their noses at others as if they are better. This treatment was starting to piss me off. It had been a long day, and I just wanted to go home and go to sleep. I debated the pros and cons of just saying screw it and calling it a day. Instead, I took a deep breath, counted to ten in my head, and resisted the urge to choke her senseless.

"Well, thank you for your time," I said and found my way back into the elevator. I gave the scowling secretary my brightest smile and pressed the button for the floor below.

When the doors closed, I stuck out my tongue and gave her the finger, proving I'm still very much a mature adult. The lift dinged, and the doors opened on the lower floor. I got out, headed for the stairs, and made my way back up to the top floor.

Easing the door open just a crack, I peeked into the waiting room. My line of sight to the front desk was unobstructed, and the snooty bat was still at her desk, standing guard over the entrance like a well-dressed gargoyle. I silently and slowly closed the door, hunkering back to try to come up with a plan. I glanced around for a fire alarm to pull. There wasn't one in the stairwell, and the sprinkler head was five feet above my head, out of my reach. So, it was unlikely I could hold my lighter up to it. I really needed to start carrying ninja smoke bombs on me. I made a mental note to pick some up on my way home.

Taking another look through the door, I noted that the secretary was on the phone again, and as luck would have it, her back was turned to the door. I took a deep breath, held it, and then darted through, making a mad but silent dash across the room, past the distracted secretary, and around the divider. Standing with my back pressed against the dividing wall, I finally let out my breath in a quiet sigh of relief.

Then, of course, my luck ran out as the exit door to the stairwell slammed shut with a loud *thud*.

My panicked brain dumped adrenaline into my system, causing my senses to reach near superhuman levels. The secretary's head snapped around to scrutinize the now-closed door. Her chair squeaked as she rose to get a better view of the lobby area.

I looked around for a place to hide. All I needed was for her to decide to check the hallway and catch me. I dashed as quickly and quietly as I could to the nearest door, jerked it open, and threw myself inside. Easing the door closed as silently as possible, I held my breath and concentrated on my hearing, trying to force my ears to listen to what was happening in the hall.

The sound of high heels clicking on the floor came through the door. Leaning against it, my forehead pressed to the cool wood, I mentally followed her footsteps as she rounded the divider and came into the hall. There were a few moments of silence as she stood and scrutinized the hallway, looking for anything out of place that would confirm nosy vampire hunters were lurking about the clean, fancy, upscale office that was not for such riffraff. I slowly counted off breaths as I waited for the click of her shoes walking away.

Something brushed against the back of my neck, and I nearly screamed.

Clamping both hands over my mouth, I spun around to see what was in the room with me. It was dark, and there were no windows. As I waited for my eyes to adjust, whatever had touched my neck this time brushed my face. Suppressing the urge to scream again, I reached out, caught whatever it was in my fist, and squeezed, trying to crush it. My mind had conjured up all sorts of creepy things it could have been, but it was only a piece of string.

I gave it a pull, and fluorescent light clicked on above my head. The room I'd ducked into was a janitor's closet, and luckily, not an occupied office or a boardroom full of people. It was in complete contrast to the fancy office outside. They were on opposite ends of the spectrum. Whereas the lobby and hall had been expensively appointed, and everything was glossy and clean, the closet was extremely barebone. The walls were still cinder block, and the floors were concrete. No fancy flooring or carpeting in here. I guess the corporate elite didn't see any sense in dolling up a room that was only used by the help.

There was surprisingly little in the room itself, aside from one of those deep utility sinks and a rolling mop bucket. There was only one set of shelves, and they were very poorly stocked. No paper towels or toilet paper, just a few cleaning chemicals and a couple of mops. I guess the cleaning staff didn't like to spend much time on this floor, and I couldn't blame them. I would want to spend as little time as possible cleaning up after people who didn't see me as human.

Once my heartbeat had returned to a mostly normal rhythm, I closed my eyes and focused on the hall outside. At first, there was only silence, but then my ears picked up the sounds of fingers typing on a keyboard. The desk troll had decided nothing had gotten past her and she'd returned to guarding the lobby while looking for poor goats to eviscerate.

I cracked the door and peered into the corridor before taking the chance to stick my head out for a better view. When the coast was clear, I slipped out quietly and eased the door closed behind me. I consulted the mental compass in my head and set off in search of the office where Baker had been thrown out the window.

I found it fairly easily. The floor layout was a basic setup of hallways and offices with numbers on the walls and names on doors. It wasn't too different from my own, but I liked mine better. Baker's office was the only one with yellow police tape on it. Two pieces crossed it from corner to corner in a big X, and in the middle of the door was a notice to stay out of an active crime scene. I ignored both of these and hunkered in front of the doorknob. It was a basic setup most offices have, a simple five-pin key lock set into the center of the knob.

Reaching into my pocket, I took out a small leather case. It looked much like a wallet, but it was longer and thinner. I flipped it open, and inside were a number of long metal tools. Lockpick sets like this were illegal unless you were a licensed locksmith. Picking a lock is nothing like what they show on TV. In the movies, they always shove two metal pieces into the lock, turn it, and the lock pops open instantly. In real life, it takes a lot longer. Even master locksmiths take five to ten minutes just to pick simple locks. While I'm not that skilled, I am lucky, and this door, while set to lock, wasn't designed as a measure to keep people out if they wanted in. That's what the building's security was for. This door was mostly meant for insurance and peace of mind.

From my pick set, I took a small rectangular piece about the size and shape of a credit card, but a bit more flexible. I slipped the card between the door and the jamb, worked it down until it slid the catch back into the base plate, and the door popped open. I gave it a light push, and it swung open easily with no noise. The room inside was a mess. Papers were strewn around, probably due to the wind coming through the giant hole in the window. The office was well appointed in earth tones, lots of dark browns, wood, and leather.

There was a large wooden desk that faced the doorway, and two squat leather chairs sat in front of it, probably for guests. One wall had a bar set with paintings hung above it. The other wall was offset with a floor-to-ceiling bookcase filled with leather-bound volumes. Aside from the large hole behind the desk, it was a very nice office, and it certainly looked like the kind of place where multi-million-dollar deals were done. I was underdressed and shabby by comparison. I was very out of place here.

As I put my tools away, I took out a pair of leather gloves and slipped them on. When you want to go snooping around places like crime scenes without leaving prints, gloves are a good idea. Most people would use disposable ones. However, this is a clear giveaway you are up to no good unless you're a cop or a doctor. Leather gloves, on the other hand, do the same job and don't look suspicious. Mine were also lined with Kevlar, making them cut-proof and adding a measure of protection.

I ducked under the tape and slipped into the room. Hot as it had been today, inside the room, it was cool. The wind at the high altitude kept the room at a cooler temperature than the rest of the building without the protection of the glass, I guessed. I made my way around the desk for a better look at the broken window.

Behind the desk lay a leather office desk chair, overturned on the floor. It was on its side, not on its back, so it was evident the poor guy hadn't just tipped over backward and gone ass-over-tea-kettle out the window. Not that *that* would have happened. These high-rise windows didn't open and were fitted with safety glass. I could've run across the room and thrown myself into the window, and all that would've happened was I bounced off it. It took a lot of force to break those things, not something an average person could do unless they were lucky or unlucky.

The window was floor-to-ceiling, just a wall of glass. It was divided into three sections. The middle one was the one Baker had gone through. It was mostly just an empty section of wall between the other two windows. Only a few large pieces of glass in the upper corners and some small fragments on the carpet were left of it now. I looked at the small pieces on the floor. Blowback. This meant the window had been shattered with some force, not just the window giving way.

As I said, physics makes fools of us all. For the glass to have sprayed back like this, it would've required the glass be shattered with such violence, it sent these shards flying in the opposite direction as the incoming energy. It's very unlikely a human could generate that kind of force.

A twinge of pain shot through my already aching skull. All this thinking, on top of a head injury, was starting to give me another headache. My brain was still foggy from last night's beating, so complex problem-solving was going to be taxing until I could get some aspirin or something to clear the cobwebs.

I picked up one of the shards and turned it in my hand. It was exactly like the larger piece in my pocket. If you looked through it, it was like normal glass. When turned sideways, the cross-section had a thin black line that ran down the middle. I ran my finger across the edge, and felt nothing but the roughness of the break.

I tossed the piece aside and eyed the open window. Maintenance hadn't had time to put anything over it and had just settled for locking the door to keep people away from the dangerous area. There was a piece of police caution tape running across the gap, but other than that, it was open to the world. I peeked over the edge and looked down. My stomach did a slow somersault, and my head swam with dizziness. I hurried away from the edge and sat with my back against the desk until it passed. Looking down from that height was a terrifying experience, and vertigo had hit me like a truck.

I stood and turned my attention to the desk. All the standard things you would expect were there: pens, papers, a leather-bound ledger, paper clips, and rubber bands. There was even a multi-line phone, but I didn't see a computer. I guess it was possible Baker didn't have one, but I doubted it. I peeked under the desk and found a power cord for a laptop. So, he did have one. It just wasn't here. That was odd. It hadn't been logged into police evidence. I hadn't seen it on the list of stuff taken from his office. There could be a dozen reasons why it wasn't on Baker's desk, but the most likely one was because whoever killed him took it. Bingo: motive. Vampires didn't care about computers, but people did.

Papers had been blown around, but not as much as I would've expected. I tried to make sense of a few of them, but between my fuzzy brain and the fact I barely have a high school education, I couldn't make heads or tails of all the corporate speak, though I'm not sure anyone is supposed to. I glanced around the office, and a blinking light caught my attention. It was a small screen on a printer, sitting on a low shelf of the bookcase.

I walked over and looked at the screen. It flashed an error message. *Page two of three. Paper jam. Check tray.* I checked the tray and found nothing. So, I popped open the machine and found a sheet of paper crumpled in the gears. I pulled at it until it came loose. The printer made a clunking noise, and it whirred as it loaded a new sheet of paper. The error message disappeared, and a new one read: *Resume printing?* I shrugged and hit the Print button. The machine hummed as it spit out the remaining page.

I looked at the crumpled and partially printed page in my hand. It was some sort of spreadsheet. Columns of numbers were divided into little boxes, but some of the lines were colored with red bars. About halfway down the page, everything just sort of faded into a smear where the jam had interrupted the printing. The printer finished and spat out the new sheet into the tray.

It was just like the other page—numbers in columns and rows, some marked with red, but a few were marked green on this page. I stuffed both into one of my pockets. I'd try to make sense of them later when I was able to think. They were probably nothing, but you never know. It's not like I was really wasting anything but time.

My attention moved to the bookshelves. I loved books and read a lot, so someone with this many couldn't be all that bad. All of the volumes were leather-bound, of different shapes and sizes. However, none of them had any titles. There were no markings to tell which book was which. Odd and needlessly confusing, in my opinion.

I reached for one of the books and pulled it off the shelf, half expecting a secret passageway to open.

The book was heavy. I turned it, and noted all the pages were gold-edged, very fancy. When I tried to open it, it wouldn't budge. There was no lock or binding. The book just wouldn't open. Thumping on it with my knuckles revealed it was a block of wood made to look like a book.

I put it back and tried another, only to get the same results. After checking a third and a fourth, I realized all the books were fakes. This bookcase was only here to look impressive, which felt like cheating to me.

"Can I help you?" came a male voice from behind me.

I jumped in surprise and nearly peed myself in terror. I turned to face the owner of the voice. The speaker was an older man, maybe in his late fifties or early sixties, but it was well-maintained aging of people who took care of themselves.

He was about the same height as I was, but something about the way he held himself made him seem taller or more imposing. His posture was better than mine, as I tend to slouch. He was dressed in an impeccable suit that probably cost more than my office building. It was a dark charcoal gray with pinstripes and creases so sharp, they looked like they could cut. It hung impossibly perfect, as though on a designer mannequin and not a human being. It was a bespoke, tailored job.

Great, I looked even more like a homeless person next to this guy.

"Um, yeah. I'm a consultant with the police investigation looking into Mr. Baker's death."

"I was under the impression they were finished for the day." He seemed less than affected by the fact one of his co-workers had just died horribly. Between the secretary and this guy, I was starting to wonder if anyone who worked in this office had a soul.

"Well, I'm just doing a final walk-through. By the way, I didn't catch your name," I replied.

"I'm Victor Baptiste, president and owner of the company and building. Mr. Baker was my business partner, and my friend."

Great, busted by the guy who could easily make this job worse. While I'd been asked to investigate by Bullard, I was playing fast and loose with several laws, and technically was trespassing on a closed crime scene. The wrong word to the wrong person, and I could find myself in trouble, off the case, in jail, or worse, out of a job. Whacking vampires is good for my bottom line, but for some reason, society frowns on the offing of bill collectors. A blood-sucking parasite is a blood-sucking parasite in my book. Baptiste looked like Max Schreck with hair plugs. His skin was waxy and pale, with piercing black eyes. He looked like a vampire who had just stepped out of the silver screen. I started to wonder if maybe...

"So, you're the big Muckity Muck? The head honcho? The boss man?"

He cocked out an immaculately manicured eyebrow.

Oh good, I was annoying him. "The Top Dog? The numero uno? El hefe? The big kahuna?"

He held up one long, thin-fingered hand, silencing my nervous babble. His fingernails screamed vampire, or maybe coke fiend. The nail on his pinkie finger looked long and sharp enough to cut an artery.

While Hollywood doesn't get vampires right most of the time, it's amazing how many vampires style themselves after the Hollywood stereotypes.

Shaking his head in obvious dismissal, he walked to the bar along the opposite wall, which was bathed in full sunlight from one of the unbroken windows. Okay, so he was just a corporate vampire, not a regular vampire. Too obvious. That would've made my job so much easier. And now I had to fish for information.

"So...what did Mr. Baker do for you?" I put the fake book back on the shelf, trying to act nonchalant and hoping we would not circle back to the legality of my presence.

"He was the CEO," he said as if that explained it.

I had no clue what a CEO does or what that means, and I was getting the feeling that was the point. No one was supposed to know what CEOs did except make way too much money and act like everyone was mad at them for no reason.

"So, what do you do here?"

"I'm the owner and president, as I have already informed you." Baptiste busied himself, making a drink from the bar.

He was showing remarkable resistance to my levels of ignorance. Most people were ready to commit homicide at this point. Hell, Benson had me out the window before I got to say one word. That's a personal record for me.

"No, I mean your company. What do you do? What do you make, or sell, or whatever?"

"Make or sell." I could swear the ghost of a smile touched his red lips.

Okay, I was amusing him. That was new and unexpected. I'm usually the only person who finds me amusing.

"We make deals, and we sell futures," His voice was a deep, rich, almost velvety purr. His words were amazingly cryptic and vague, making me think I might've bumped into the actual devil, or the weird creepy shopkeeper from that Stephen King book.

He stared at me with deep black eyes as if looking through me or into me, and it creeped me out.

"At B&B Acquisitions, we facilitate the mergers and acquisitions of other companies. Donald was a financial wizard with accounting. He handled the finances and offsets. He would oversee the transitions and trim the excess fat by removing redundancies in staffing personnel and assets."

I nodded along as though I understood. Like the spreadsheets, I didn't comprehend any of those words in that order.

"Did Mr. Baker have any enemies? You know, anyone who wanted to kill him?"

This got a laugh out of the man.

"He was a CEO, my boy. His enemies were many. Mostly the rabble-rousing mediocrity who can't stand businessmen earning a dollar. Politicians blaming us for all the world's evils. Communists, socialists, every loud college kid with a megaphone out to make a name for themselves as an activist. It would be a shorter list of people who didn't want him dead." He smirked as he sipped his drink.

"Well, how about just the people who could get into the building or his office?" I asked.

"None that I know of. We are the only two people with offices on this floor. Our security and secretary, none of whom are malcontents. I suppose he could have let some third party in

I didn't know about, but that is...unlikely." The way the man spoke made me think of Vincent Price. Seriously, what kind of character was this guy, or were all stupidly wealthy businessmen just full-blown Howard Hughes types?

"Outside of business, what about his family, wife, girlfriend, mistress...male hookers?" Now, I was just looking for a way out of the conversation because this was quickly starting to resemble a scene from a bad cable movie where the serial killer murders the oblivious, busty blonde.

"Donald was not a family man as far as I knew. As for his dalliances, well, he was...self-sufficient."

The way the sunlight played on his pale features made dark circles appear under his eyes, giving his face a thin pinched-corpse appearance. Something about him really didn't sit right with me in the pit of my stomach. Somewhere in the back of my brain, an alarm bell was going off I couldn't place.

"It's late, shouldn't you be going, Mr....pardon, I didn't get your name." He smiled like a cat cornering a particularly fat and juicy mouse.

Yep, time to go.

"Oh, yeah, look at the time." I mimed looking at a watch on my wrist that didn't exist. "I have to report in with the other investigators."

"You do that," he purred and watched me a little too closely as I left the office.

As I headed back to the lobby, replaying the conversation with Baptiste, the hawk-like secretary came around the wall dividing the lobby from the hall. With her was a security guard. She pointed at me and said something to the guard. As he walked towards me, I could tell just from looking at him he was going to be trouble, and not the you-broke-the-rules kind of trouble.

He was short and stocky, the kind of build when you're insecure about your height, so you compensate by bulking up, but never lose the gut. The way he walked and the look on his face told me he was one of those guys who wanted to be a cop, but failed the psychological exam, and rent-a-cop was the only job he could get. I would've laid money that he spends his off days running around the woods with other guys just like him, playing army man and preparing to fight the commies while yelling *Wolverines*!

"Hey, asshole. You don't belong here," he yelled at me as he approached.

While I have issues with authority, I have nothing but contempt for bullies pretending to be authorities or hiding behind a badge. I ignored his yelling as I kept walking towards him, knowing what was going to happen next.

He pulled something from his belt, and with a flick of his wrist, the baton clicked open. I could see in his eyes he was looking for any excuse to use it to tool up on me. I was too tired and sore to deal with another beating, especially not from this little dumbass.

"Hey, I'm talking to you! Don't ignore me, you—"

As he reached for my collar with his left hand, I shifted my weight to my right side, and using my left, I swept his to my left and followed through by grasping his wrist and pulling him off balance. I put my right hip into his waist, using it to send him crashing face-first into the floor. I grabbed the back of his head with my other hand as he fell, and used the inertia of the fall plus my body weight to slam his skull into the ground.

I could've ended it there. He was down, and his ego was thoroughly checked. However, when I do something, I tend to make sure it's done. I cranked back on his left arm, putting my body weight into it until the elbow joint made a loud popping noise as though someone had uncorked a large bottle of wine.

The guard's arm was now bent in the opposite way. The joint was dislocated, but not broken. It would heal, but he wouldn't be beating up on anyone anytime soon.

The secretary stood in silent shock, her jaw hanging open at the sight of the downed guard.

I climbed off the jerk, leaving him lying unconscious on the ground. I tipped her a wave as I walked past, leaving her stunned and silent.

I whistled *We'll Meet Again* as I boarded the elevator and thumbed the ground floor button, happy to be out of there, on my way home to a soft bed and a bottle of aspirin.

Chapter 6

I swung into the office the next morning. I was still stiff and sore, but a night of rest and pain relievers had turned everything down to a dull ache. My ribs still throbbed, but my head was clear and trying to piece together the weirdness of yesterday. Hopefully, today would yield some answers, as I had too many questions and no clue where to start. I pulled up short, and the bottom dropped out of my stomach.

Bullard and Benson stood around Anita's desk, talking and laughing. Wonderful, there was no way this wouldn't turn out bad.

"Morning, Halson," Bullard said when I closed the door.

"You look like shit," Benson said around a mouthful of doughnut.

I gave her an eye roll. Anita would bring in boxes of doughnuts from time to time, and the two cops were helping themselves.

I made my way over to the box on the desk, grabbed one, and took a big bite. Ugh, not a doughnut. I spat out the mouthful of some kind of bagel.

"What savage buys bagels?" I tossed the rest into the trash.

"Don't you go wasting perfectly good food, boy," Anita scolded.

I dug out an actual doughnut this time and ate half of it in two bites.

"I'm sure these *fine* officers appreciate a healthy breakfast, unlike some people." She winked at Bullard when she said *fine*, putting emphasis on the word.

I finished my doughnut and grabbed another. "So, what brings the Philly PD down to our humble little hole in the wall?"

"Just checking up on your investigation yesterday," Bullard said. "Wondering what your opinion on it is."

"Like I said yesterday, it's not a vampire attack. The marks on the body were not vampire marks. While I can't explain the lack of blood and the window is suspicious, but it's not inexplicable. The glass is strong, but if you use a glass breaker or damage it, you can break it."

"What about the blood and bite marks? Clearly those are signs of an attack," Alex interjected as she selected another doughnut.

Way to feed the cop stereotype.

"Halson was right yesterday. The coroner's report said those marks were made by a large gauge needle, something like what's used in a blood transfusion. They were clean and sterile. Real vampires bite and tear like dogs with a piece of meat. There were no other marks that weren't made postmortem."

"But what about the missing blood?" Alex asked as though Bullard's explanation wasn't enough for her.

"That's actually more telling than the marks." I shrugged.

"What do you mean?" Alex put her hands on her hips.

"Vampires, no matter how preternatural they are, started as human beings, and they still have human stomachs. The average human stomach can only hold about four liters at the most, but the average human body contains five liters of blood. So, a single vampire cannot drain every single drop of blood. There would need to be more than one vampire. If there *was* more than one vampire, there would be more bites, and as Bullard says, 'vampire bites are nasty and brutal'." I poured myself a cup of coffee and dunked my doughnut before taking another bite.

"It's creepy you know how much blood a stomach can hold," Alex said, clearly annoyed her theory was being shot down so thoroughly. "Okay, so a vampire can't drink all the blood in a person's body. So, he was clearly killed somewhere else and dumped out the window. That just means the blood is wherever he was originally killed."

"To remove every single drop of blood, like what was done with Donald Baker, requires a special pump like what's used by morticians or in kidney dialysis," Bullard added. "Halson is right. Vampires, while supernatural monsters, still face some of the same limits as humans. That kind of suction can't be done by a human mouth, and again, the marks are clearly not vampire bites."

"Great," I exclaimed with sarcasm, "that means I'm done. Pay me, get out, and stop eating my doughnuts."

"Hey, watch your mouth." Anita swatted me on the back of the head. "I won't have you talking that way to such an upstanding man of the law. He works hard keeping us safe and needs all the energy he can get. Sugar, you can have as much want." She tipped him another wink.

Anita has had a thing for Bullard since they met, so every time she's around him, she flirts shamelessly, despite him being married. It's harmless and I found it funny.

He smiled slyly and ignored her come-ons. "I want you to stay on the case for now."

"Why? No vampire, no need for me. I mean, if you want to keep paying my bills, it's your dime, but I don't see how I'm gonna be of any help."

"Whoever did this wants us to think it was a vampire attack, so as long as you're snooping about, they'll think we fell for it."

"Leaving you guys free to search for the real culprit, banking on them slipping up because they'll think their ploy worked," I finished for him. "You know, I really don't like being bait."

"Don't think of it as bait, Halson. Think of it as being a diversion," Alex chimed in.

"Wow, I didn't know cops knew fancy words like diversion, but it's not gonna work."

"What do you mean it's not gonna work?" Ignoring my snide comments, her hands returned to her hips.

"People don't believe in vampires and the preternatural. They're gonna think I'm a nut." I sighed. "And aside from not being a cop, I really don't fit in with the white-collar crowd."

This was an understatement, and all three of them gave me a head-to-toe looking over.

Today, I was wearing beat-up motorcycle boots, faded jeans with one worn knee and a hole below a back pocket. My shirt was a dark blue plaid with the sleeves rolled up, worn over a t-shirt bearing the image of Bart Simpson and the words "Don't have a cow, man." I'd left my duster in the car because of the heat, not really needing it to cover my gun, thanks to the open button shirt which achieved the same function. The cotton didn't offer the same level of protection or coverage as the heavy canvas coat, but it was really hot outside. According to the news, it was going to be another record breaker.

"I swear, Halson," Alex said in disgust. "You dress like a five-year-old."

"A very comfortable five-year-old." I gave her my shit-eating grin, complete with a mouthful of doughnut.

She rolled her eyes again. "Like I said, a five-year-old."

"There was also a report of a suspicious person in the building, and one of the security guards ended up in the hospital with a concussion and a severely dislocated elbow joint." Bullard interrupted our childish little exchange. He could only tolerate our immature back and forth for so long before having to step in. At times, I think he might be afraid it could devolve into hair pulling or someone getting a bug dropped down the back of their shirt.

Sometimes, I think he might be right.

"You wouldn't happen to know anything about that, would you?" He gave me one of his hard expressions.

Bullard was a very imposing man, and it's not just his size, even though that's part of it. It's his eyes. When he gets set on something and it's time to get serious, they turn into piercing searchlights that feel as if they can penetrate straight to your very soul. He's got to be absolutely terrifying in an interrogation room. Of course, I fight supernatural creatures who could easily tear me in half and eat me body and soul, which means I've gotten pretty good at not letting them see how much they make me want to wet my pants. Thus, I'm pretty good at holding up under Bullard's scrutiny.

I stuffed more doughnut into my mouth so I wouldn't have to answer, and shrugged. Lying to the police is a felony. Technically, I wasn't lying. Even though this was more along the lines of a friendly meeting, not a police inquiry, and Bullard hadn't directly asked me if I was responsible, but cops are still cops. There is no off the record. Admitting to anything in front of a cop is generally a bad idea.

Law enforcement is one of those careers that's more of a lifestyle choice than a job. Even after they clock out for the day and take off the uniform, they're still cops and still on the job. It's not unlike what I do. Even when I'm not getting paid or hunting a vampire down, I'm still a vampire hunter. I can't just turn a blind eye because it's not "work hours." It's who I am. It's the same with Bullard and Benson. They may be smiling and relaxed, but they were still cops, and I can respect that.

Even though Bullard was an old-grizzled vet while Benson was relativity young and experienced, both would still be cops long after they retired their shields. Heck, probably even after they died, they would still be cops.

Oh God, that is a depressing idea for the afterlife.

"Try to stay out of trouble." Bullard sighed. "We can't afford to...indulge shenanigans. These guys have enough money and clout to bury us in lawsuits."

"What do they actually do?" I asked through another mouthful of doughnut.

"Mergers and acquisitions," Alex responded.

That was about as clear as mud, and I understood it just as little as I had last night when Baptiste had said it. I barely managed to finish high school, forget about college. So, the inner workings of corporate America are beyond a dullard like me.

"I have no clue what that means."

"It's a fancy way of saying corporate raiders. They buy up or merge with another company, and then they gut the company's pensions, benefits, and other finances under the pretext of cutting costs, then run it into the ground to sell off the assets. They get rich and make money by destroying and cannibalizing other companies, and then they write it off as a loss to get a bailout from the government."

"That doesn't exactly sound legal."

"Well, sadly it is. They use loopholes and hoard their money in offshore accounts. Even when they do something that's illegal, they don't end up in jail unless their victims happen to also be affluent rich people, as well. Stealing from the poor is totally legal." Venom had crept into Alex's voice. That chip on her shoulder was waving a big red flag which made me curious.

"Say, Alex, what did you do before you got bounced into the PSIC unit?" I asked.

"I was in white-collar crime."

Her tone of voice carried a hint of danger as if daring me to make something of it. I had a better idea of how Alex, an idealistic rookie with no street experience, ended up in the starting lineup of the loser's club. No doubt, she'd stepped on the toes of some high-class suit, and they'd used the power and privilege to end her career before it had begun. I once read somewhere that the world has teeth, and it can bite you with them anytime it wants, and it had bitten Alex. It bites us all, just in different ways. Life is unfair, and it seems like the least deserving people get it the most.

"We aren't here to judge whether or not they lack a moral compass. Our job is to find the murderer," interrupted Bullard. "So, we have to watch our step. This killer was smart enough to try to confuse us with false evidence. We don't know what other tricks they may have up their sleeve."

"Okay, Dad, I'll be careful with the car and not take Susie Q up to lovers' lane."

"I'm serious, Halson. Keep a low profile on this. Be just visible enough for people to know you're there and why, without causing trouble."

He gave me is no-nonsense glare, and I put up both my hands in surrender.

"Fine, let's do this your way. I'll try to stay out of trouble." I even held up three fingers in a boy scout salute, and for once, I meant it.

"Alright, we've got to get down to the station, but I've left word with the patrolmen on site to give you the same access as the investigators. But remember, you aren't a cop, Halson, you need to be careful."

"I get it." I sighed, finishing off my doughnut.

He seemed satisfied with that, so he and Alex thanked Anita, and left the office.

As I watched them go, I couldn't help but feel as if this case was gonna be more trouble than it's worth.

Anita broke through my brooding. "I don't know how or why that man puts up with you." She shook her head as she put the box of doughnuts away. Her red curls bounced and swayed as her head shook.

"Why did you take this job?" I asked, cocking an eyebrow.

"Because I couldn't get a job anywhere else, and you were the only person dumb enough to pay me.".

"Bingo," I said. "They have no other choice. Before hiring me, PSIC just muddled along with no clue what they were doing, and it's only thanks to Bullard they didn't suffer more casualties. Most of their guys have never actually seen a real live monster. Heck, I doubt Benson has ever actually encountered a hardened criminal, forget facing off with a vampire. She still thinks this is all some game."

"She seems like one tough cookie. I mean, you don't get to be the department head's number two without earning a few hard knocks, especially for a woman."

"Yeah, that hard-nosed act is really convincing when you come out of a soft division like white-collar crimes. It's not hard to intimidate accountants and bankers. Street criminals gamble with their lives every day on false bravado, acting tougher than they are. Her first time getting knocked down a peg or two is gonna be rough, and I do not envy the guy who earns her wrath."

"Well, if you ask me, you two just need to get a motel room and do the nasty."

"Jesus Christ!" I nearly choked on a mouthful of coffee.

Every now and then, I forget Anita is from the projects. She lures me in with her sweet old lady routine and then sucker punches me with ghetto sass when I let my guard down. I'm pretty sure she gets a kick out of getting the better of me.

I grabbed a couple of napkins and tried to wipe most of the spilled coffee off my shirt. It's not like I hadn't thought about it, but Alex was out of my league, and I didn't really have a lot of experience with women. And when I say I don't have a lot of experience with women, I mean none. When I was a teenager full of hormones, there'd been some effort at socializing with the fairer sex. However, nothing came from it, as most of my focus had been dedicated to turning my blind hate and youthful rage into becoming a hunter so I could seek revenge.

As romantic as that notion was, all it did was leave me with a lonely life and a trail of bodies, both friend and foe, in my wake. My love life had been one of those casualties. Sometimes, I wondered how my parents did it. How had they managed to have a normal life and raise a family, knowing the horrors that waited around every corner? Considering what had happened, maybe they were wrong.

"Do me a favor while I'm out. Look up a glass expert for me, someone who does windows, and try to find someone who can make heads or tails of this." I tossed the crumpled-up papers I had taken from Baker's office last night.

Anita picked them up and leafed through. It was clear from her expression she couldn't understand it either. "What is it?"

"Dunno. Maybe nothing, maybe something, but it couldn't hurt to find out. If nothing else, it will give me a better idea of what they're doing there." And with that, I grabbed my car keys, checked to make sure my gun was loaded, and headed back to the scene of the crime.

Chapter 7

If the morning had started off rocky, the rest of my day was worse. Aside from the heat just making everyone miserable, none of them had been in any mood to talk to the shabby, out-of-place investigator. The cops at the front had let me pass without really acknowledging me. The hawk-like girl at the front desk had given me the same dismissive look she had the other day. Apparently, her opinion of me had not changed. It was probably lower now that she couldn't just call security and have me thrown out. Speaking of security, the lack of it was rather odd. I didn't see a single guard.

There were the obvious cameras, as you would expect in an office building. Their dark little bubbles were dotted around in key places here and there, but there were no actual humans. Beyond the guy I had hospitalized the night before, there had to be more personnel for a building this size. Granted, it wasn't a bank and didn't handle any actual money that I knew of, but still, wouldn't you need actual people?

I wondered how many people you would need to guard a building this size. There had to be a central control room for the cameras and at least a couple of guys to walk the floors. Then I remembered I hadn't seen a janitor, either, but I'm sure they're probably more active after hours. Don't want the riffraff lower class mingling with the pressed white collars of the yuppie workers.

I am not too proud to admit that my original judgment was wrong. Most of the people I could get to acknowledge me were as tired and downtrodden as I was, just wearing more boring clothing. I spent the morning riding the elevator up and down, occasionally sticking my head out to check the floor. Every now and then, I would get out and explore.

I tried talking to a few people, but I didn't get much. The longest conversation was with a woman who'd been smoking on a balcony. She'd been wearing your typical office wardrobe, or as far as I knew, it was. She wore a crisp, clean white blouse and a short, black pencil skirt. She held a cigarette in one red-nailed hand as her brunette hair whipped about in the wind. We were a couple dozen floors up, and I had no clue how she'd managed to keep her cigarette lit.

When I tried to strike up a conversation, she asked if I was a cop. I had avoided the question, trying to sidestep and deflect. She curtly replied that if the cops wanted anything from her, they would need a warrant. She had snuffed out her cigarette butt with a finality that signaled our talk was over, and she sashayed away.

That was pretty much the same way every interaction went. I would approach, and they would rebuff me with variations of "I'm busy," "I don't know," or "Not my department." Some were a bit cold, others were just annoyed, but most were just tired and wanted to be anywhere else.

Until I met Lenny, and I struck pay dirt.

Just before lunchtime, I'd found my way into a break room with a couple of tables and chairs. Counters lined the wall, except where there was a fridge and a soda machine. A microwave and a coffee maker sat on the counters next to them. I figured the fridge looked suspicious and decided to investigate. You never know where a vampire might be hiding.

While I had my head buried in the cold relief, looking for evil sandwiches no one would miss, I spotted a sub sandwich that looked like it possessed a blackened soul. Only by passing through my mighty colon could it be properly purified. Being the valiant hero that I am, I decided I would have to make the sacrifice. I took the sandwich out and unwrapped it. It was a Philly cheese steak with all the fixins.

"It's not nice to steal other people's lunches," said a voice out of nowhere.

I almost jumped out of my skin. I looked around to find one of those nebbish office worker types sitting alone at one of the tables. He wore the typical white shirt and khaki pants that seemed to be standard in office environments. His glasses were thick, dark-frame jobs which further made him resemble a nerd. His receding hairline and thick porno mustache made me think he might not be allowed within fifty feet of a school.

Yeah, it was a little mean, but seriously, if you have a mustache like that, you know what people are gonna think of you.

"Well, I'm with the police looking into Mr. Baker's, um, accident." I wasn't really sure how much I should be telling people.

"You don't look like a cop," he replied.

Wow, I wonder what gave me away. "True. I'm an investigator, and looking for evidence."

"In a sandwich?" He wasn't buying into my subterfuge.

"We won't know until I have sent it to the lab to be analyzed," I stated. "And by lab, I mean my stomach." I sat at the table across from the guy and bit into the sandwich.

"That's Becky's sandwich." His voice had a nasally almost whiny quality to it. It was mildly irritating.

I had an odd compulsion to wedgie him and shove him in a locker. "I guess I owe Becky a sandwich. Who's Becky?"

"She's our supervisor. And she's kind of a bitch."

"Well, I won't tell her if you don't." I gave him a wink "So, what is it we do here?"

"We do the accounting for most of the companies in the building, but we are mostly in-house for B&B Acquisitions."

He picked at his food, a lackluster assortment of carrot sticks, what looked like a bland bologna sandwich, and a vanilla pudding cup. The most exciting thing about it was probably the mayo and mustard on the sandwich. It made my diet of ramen and leftovers seem downright extravagant by comparison.

"So, what's your name, guy?" I tried to get him to open up to me some more. We'd bonded over mutual disdain for the boss, and after a whole day of strikeouts, I could use a win.

Hopefully, I could pump him for more information. As an employee, he would have the inside track on at least some of the office gossip. Inside politics and rumors, the cops wouldn't ask about or they wouldn't think to divulge. Small details could slip through the cracks, but could lead to real leads.

"Lenny, Lenny Coogan, accounts receivables." He offered me his hand and I shook it. It was clammy and limp. Kinda gross, but I resisted the urge to wipe my own hand off on my shirt, so I slipped it beneath the table and wiped it on my pants leg instead.

"So, Lenny, what's the word around the water cooler?" I asked. "What are people saying about what happened?"

"About Mr. Baker's death?" He screwed his face in consideration, the effect not doing him any favors. "No one is really talking about it much. We're in the middle of a company-wide internal audit that needs to be finished by the end of the quarter.

So, we're pretty slammed, and everyone is grumpy over the new changes in the incentive programs."

"Incentive programs?" I cocked an eyebrow, imagining a cavalcade of rewards for bilking little old ladies out of their life savings.

"Yeah, they eliminated pretty much all but one of them now." He picked morosely at his sad sandwich.

"How's that work?" I had about as much of an idea about his world as he had of mine.

"Well, they started these incentives to get employees to participate in programs that would allow the company to be entitled to certain state tax breaks." He sipped his diet soda.

I still had no idea what he was talking about, and it must have shown on my face, so he elaborated.

"The company would give out bonuses to every employee who participated in the programs. Things like recycling and carpooling, mostly green initiative policies that the city was trying to get everyone to follow. For every program you did, you got a cash bonus, usually between twenty to fifty bucks, depending on the program. So, you could make a pretty nice little bonus each month for relatively little effort. In return, the company got a tax break."

"So, what changed?"

"Change of administrations in D.C., the green tax breaks were replaced with corporate tax breaks. So, they've been shutting down the incentive programs. The only thing left now is the monthly blood drive. I don't know anyone who likes it, but it's a free cookie and fifty bucks."

My ears pricked up at the mention of a blood drive. They use needles to extract blood and Donald Baker had needle marks on his neck.

"When was the last blood drive?" I asked, playing my hunch.

"Last weekend, I think? I was away to visit my mom in the hospital," he said. "I usually work late on Tuesdays and Thursdays so I can take off early and drive up state to visit her at their facility."

"Where do they do that? Do they have a Bloodmobile come around or do you have to go downtown for that?" I prodded.

"Oh, uh, no. They have a clinic here in the building."

I blinked. I wasn't expecting that. I'd hoped it was done on site, that way one of the Bloodmobile people could be the suspect. Bullard would've been happy when I told him, but to have a clinic onsite? What kind of place was this where they had a clinic inside their building?

"Why do they have a clinic?" I asked.

"I think it was a laboratory at one time. They did independent testing and stuff for various companies in the city. Nothing too technical, mostly like drug tests and stuff like that. I know because, when I first started here, they did all the drug tests in-house. When the business shut down, they sort of turned it into a nurse's office for the other companies in the business, but it's owned by B&B. So, once a month, the blood bank staff come in for a couple days and people go donate. I don't go much because I don't like needles."

"Where is this clinic?" All sorts of ideas and theories were running through my head. I hadn't expected this windfall. If things kept breaking my way, I could wrap up this disaster before quitting time, and then knock off to treat myself to a pizza or something to celebrate another case closed.

"It's a few floors up, but it's not open now." He returned to his paltry lunch.

"Will you look at the time!" I held up my wrist doing my invisible watch gimmick again. "It's almost lunchtime." I wolfed down the rest of the sandwich and stood.

"But you just ate?" Lenny said, confused, as I headed towards the door of the break room.

I waved one hand over my shoulder without looking back. "Keep it real, Lenny."

Chapter 8

I headed back to the elevators and checked the building directory. Lenny had been right, and I found the clinic listed just a few floors up.

Catching an empty lift, I headed up. I hummed along happily with the music as I ascended. Today was turning out much better than I'd thought it was going to.

Getting out on the floor, I was greeted by a mostly darkened hallway. Which made sense, given no one was supposed to be here. I'd figured there would at least be a nurse or someone, but luckily, no one was, which left me free to roam at my leisure. I still kept my ears open just in case, but the floor seemed totally silent.

After a bit of casting about, I found a door marked Blood Drive. It was just a piece of printer paper taped to the door. The door itself was plain wood with a frosted window set into it.

I paused and strained my hearing, focusing on the other side of the door. Nothing, dead silence.

I tried the door, locked. No big. I dropped to my knees in front of the knob. It was a simple six tumbler. I took out my locksmith's pouch, selected two picks, and inserted them into the lock. Even with a simple one like this and as practiced as I was at picking them, it still took me a good five minutes before it sprang open.

I slipped the tools back into my pocket and opened the door. It revealed a waiting room that was the typical kind you'd find in any doctor's office. Bland décor in muted earth tones, grays, and false wood grain. The chairs were cloth covered and not the most comfortable, but also not the worst things around.

There were outdated magazines stacked on side tables. An empty closet was next to the door. Across the room was a check-in window. The glass was heavy and reinforced. Honestly, where was the trust these days? It was like they were trying to keep people out. Next to the check-out window was another door. It was clearly the entrance to the inner sanctum and probably where they did the actual bloodletting.

There was just one small problem, it was locked. Unlike the front door, this one was an electronic lock. It had a nine-digit keypad. If I was MacGyver, I would use drywall dust and a piece scotch tape to figure out the combination. I am definitely *not* MacGyver, and that always bugged me, anyways. I mean, even if you knew the numbers, you still didn't know the order, and what if they used the same number twice?

The lock hadn't beaten me. I was lucky it was one of those doors with the lever style handles instead of a normal knob. I returned to the closet, and my luck was still in as I found a wire coat hanger. I twisted the hanger and straightened it out. Then I kicked off one of my boots and pulled out the lace. I tied one end of the lace into a loop and then hooked it over one end of the hanger. I slid my improvised lever arm under the door. I wiggled it around trying to get it over the door handle. After a few frustrating attempts, the lace caught. I pulled on the other end and watched as the handle on my side slowly dipped. The door popped open, and I triumphantly re-laced my boot and put it back on.

I pushed my way into the back room. It was sterile, but a slight smell of bleach and antiseptic still hung in the air. With no windows to let in light, the inner room was almost pitch black. I used the light coming through the door to find the switch, and was nearly blinded as the brilliant bulbs snapped on.

When my vision had returned, I looked around. The room was mostly white and very sterile. The counters, floors, and walls were spotless. This made the recliners look even more out of place. There were three of them, all the same color of blue. The material was a sort of soft, crushed velvet. Next to each was a small metal side table. There was also a rolling stool the nurse undoubtedly used when drawing blood.

Dropping into the nearest recliner, I pulled the release lever and kicked up my feet as I leaned back. I stared at the ceiling and let my mind wander. There was nothing I saw that could indicate a murder took place here. Even though there was still the scent of bleach, it was a medical room, meaning they probably cleaned with bleach and sterilized all the time. I had no doubt the needles here would match the size of the punctures on Baker. But how to prove it? That was the six million dollar question.

If you were gonna murder someone, this was the place to do it. The tiled floor would clean easy, and there was a large freezer where you could stash the body. The freezer was probably where they kept the blood once it had been drawn and was awaiting transport to a hospital or wherever.

Then, an idea hit me. If I had been the killer, why waste the blood?

You have the victim in the chair and incapacitated, because I doubted Baker would've just let someone jab needles into him and drain his blood. If the victim was already here, why not just harvest the blood and save yourself the cleanup? That would make sense if the killer was one of the blood drive staff. It didn't answer the question of why, though. What motive could they have? Maybe selling the blood on the black market? I didn't have enough knowledge in that area to know if that was even a thing.

And there was still the problem of why they threw him out a window. Seemed like a lot of work to cart a body down to the clinic, drain his blood, then drag him back up to the office, and toss him out the window. Unless he was already in the clinic when he'd been killed. That seemed to fit better. It still didn't explain the window, either. Why throw the guy out the window? It seemed kind of public and overly theatrical.

The only way I could get it to make sense was if they'd wanted the death to go public. They'd wanted the cops to be called, and looking like a vampire attack meant they either wanted to confuse the police, or they knew about the PSIC unit, and dressing it up would muddy the waters to make it easier for them to get away.

I didn't know which I liked less. A killer who was clever, or a killer who was in the know on the preternatural stuff.

I had gotten too comfy and lost in thought, so I didn't hear someone come in until the door opened.

The door swung open, my attention snapped to, and I sat up.

I let out a low curse as I realized who came through. It was the guard I'd knocked out last night, and he did *not* look happy to see me. Which was fair, as I was none too pleased to see him, either.

He was sporting two black eyes, and there was a whistling noise every time he breathed. Apparently, his nose had broken when his face collided with the floor, helped along by me. There was a sling on his left arm. It hadn't been broken, but it had been hyperextended to the point that the joint had been reversed. Whoever had reset it had done a good job if all it needed was the sling. And he must've been on some good painkillers to take that level of damage and still come to work.

Me, I would have taken the week off. Granted, I'd gotten pretty banged up myself just the other day, and my body was still stiff and sore, but I don't really get the option of taking the day off. When I skip work, people get killed by vampires. Now, if I had a cushy job like babysitting office workers all day, I wouldn't be letting my sick days pile up. So, kudos to him for sticking it out and showing up for work.

He slipped his arm out of the sling as he walked towards me. His eyes blazed as his face twisted in anger. With his right hand, he pulled out his collapsing baton and flicked it open. I guess he didn't learn from last time. Though, I was pretty glad he wasn't carrying a gun.

"Let's see how tough you think you are when you can't sucker punch me." He screamed as he lunged.

I dove out of the chair just as the baton came down with a loud *whack* on the recliner's seat. I leapt to my feet and spun around to find him coming at me again. As he swung, I tried to back up, but my legs became tangled in the rolling stool I'd failed to notice.

I raised my arms to cover my head, and the blow landed across my left forearm with a dull *thud*. A muted roar of pain shot up my arm, and my fingers started to tingle. The force of the blow, and tripping over the stool, sent me sprawling on the floor. I tried to catch myself, but my numb left arm was all but useless, and I busted my lip open as my face collided with the floor. While face-down, he brought his weapon down across the back of my shoulders. A bar of heat spread across my back as he wound up for another shot.

Pushing off with my right hand, I was able to roll out of the way just as the baton came down again. It hit the floor with an ear-splitting *crack*, and the tile it struck shattered into a spiderweb pattern. That had been aimed at the back of my head.

He wasn't trying to beat me up as payback for humiliating him. He was trying to kill me.

I kicked out and managed to catch him in the knee. It didn't knock him off his feet as I had planned, but it bought me some much-needed time and space to scramble to my feet and make an attempt for the door.

Unfortunately, he recovered at the same time and made to intercept me. I pulled up short at the last second, and the baton swept down, missing the tip of my nose by a hair's breadth. I stumbled backward until the counter stopped me. My right hand bumped against a glass container of band-aids. I hucked it at the guard's head, forcing him to try and dodge it.

While he was off balance, I tackled him low, wrapping my arms around one of his legs and then yanking upwards and backward with all of my strength. As he fell over backward, he managed to get in one good lick across the side of my face. My ear seemed to explode as a stripe of white-hot pain blossomed on my left cheek, causing my eyes to water.

Being off balance and mid-fall, he hadn't managed to get much power behind it, and it was little better than a glancing blow. It still hurt like a bitch, and anger to surged in me. I was done trying to be nice. If he wanted to fight, then I'd give him a fight. Using my body weight, I drove my open hand into his throat, catching his windpipe right in the webbing between my thumb and forefinger.

His eyes bugged, and he let out a hacking gurgle of surprise as he found himself suddenly unable to breathe through a crushed throat.

If I'd wanted to kill him, the blow could have been lethal. Instead, I followed up with a swift elbow across his jaw.

He swung the baton wildly in a vain attempt to hit me, but I was on top and in control. I caught his wrist, and using the baton for leverage, twisted it, stripping the baton from him. It clattered to the floor, with a loud metallic *clang*.

He swung at me with his left fist, but I managed to catch it, and this time, I didn't show any mercy. I wasn't content with just dislocating his arm this time. I rolled forward off him, all while maintaining my grip on his arm, using all my body weight to torque his wrist. It made a satisfying, dry snapping sound as the bones in his wrist broke.

He let out a howl of pain and clasped his wrist to his chest. It bent at an odd angle. It didn't matter how many painkillers he was on. Bone pain was different from nerve pain, and there aren't a lot of medications that can do much more than dull it a bit. I'd experienced physical pain and suffering most of my adolescent life, and it had made me a harder person. Here, this pretend tough guy was rolling on the ground, crying over a silly broken wrist.

My roll maneuver had put me more or less back on my feet, ready to continue the fight. Upon seeing the guy reduced to such a pathetic sight, I knew the fight was over. I walked back into the waiting room and slumped against a wall to catch my breath.

Now that the adrenaline rush was wearing off, I was tired. My hands were still shaking, and I was all jittery. I nearly wet myself when the main door to the clinic slammed open, and two male uniformed cops entered the room with guns drawn.

I put both of my hands up as I identified myself. They let me slowly take out my pass that identified who I was, even though they kept their guns trained on me the whole time.

I still ended up handcuffed, and they put me in the back of a cop car downstairs while the idiot was hauled off by an ambulance. I sat there for what felt like an hour, and I must have nodded off at some point.

I was jolted awake by Bullard knocking on the window. He opened the door for me and let me out.

I leaned on the car as he undid the cuffs.

"I told you to stay out of trouble," Bullard growled as he handed the cuffs to a patrolman.

"I was. That asshole attacked me." The side of my face was killing me. I think the bone had been bruised, and it felt like there may have been some swelling under the eye. My vision wasn't quite right on my left side.

"The building security was alerted when you broke into the clinic." Bullard inspected the imprint on my left cheek and my busted lip. "That looks pretty nasty. Do you need to see someone about it?"

I shrugged. It was nice to know he was concerned for my well-being, but I didn't need him to mother me.

"No, it's not as bad as it looks." Though the distorted vision did bother me a bit. I wasn't going to let Bullard know the chump had nearly rolled me. "The guy attacked me with no warning. Technically, I didn't *break* anything. I just sort of let myself through some locked doors. Yeah, maybe I wasn't supposed to be there, but the guy went straight to eleven and tried to kill me."

"I know. I looked at the security tapes before coming to talk to you. It's a pretty clear case of assault with a deadly weapon. He wasn't holding back, and you could've been killed." The big man took a bottle of aspirin out of his pocket and shook out a couple for me.

I took the pills happily and slugged them back with a drink from a water bottle.

"I don't remember seeing any cameras," I said once I had swallowed the aspirin. I was wracking my brain, and I don't think I saw a single camera on that floor. There hadn't been any on the top floor, either. At least, not that I noticed yesterday.

"They were hidden cameras put in when they took over the laboratory floor. They didn't want people upset over their medical privacy, but at the same time, they needed to monitor medical supplies. Not that they keep narcotics in there, but from what I understand, some of the supplies and equipment can be valuable." He flipped through the little note pad that he kept in his jacket. "The whole thing was captured on video. You want to press charges?"

"Hell yeah, I want to press charges! Psycho nearly took my head off," I exclaimed.

Bullard nodded, making more notes.

"I'll make sure the PSIC Unit presses charges on your behalf. It'll help to keep this out of the papers."

I rolled my eyes. I guess Bullard didn't want to get any grief from his higher-ups if people found out the city was paying wild lunatics to hunt monsters for them.

"There weren't any of those hidden cameras on the top floor where Baker's office was, were there?" I was hoping I'd get lucky, and no one had bothered to check with security.

"No such luck. It was one of the first things we checked. There are no cameras anywhere in the top floor offices." He sighed and put his pad back into his jacket. "What were you doing on that floor anyways?"

"I found out from one of the employees they do monthly blood drives, and they all take place in that clinic. I would bet you dollars to doughnuts the needles they use match the puncture marks on your dead guy's neck." Then, an idea hit me. "Hey, Bullard, any way you can find where the blood is sent from here?"

"Yeah probably, why?"

"If you can find the last batch sent, test it against your victim's DNA."

"What, are you thinking our pretend vampire is really a nurse stealing blood?" His bushy eyebrows knotted.

"Dunno, maybe. I'm not sure there's a black market for things like that, but it fits."

"There is a black market for everything," he replied.

Well, that was quite a depressing notion. I was having visions of people walking around with a couple pints of someone else's blood. I wondered how you even shopped for something like that. Dozen eggs, a gallon of milk, a quart of blood, toilet paper. Ugh, creepy.

"It still doesn't explain why they tossed him out a window, but at least it's a lead," I said.

"Every little bit helps, so we take what we can get." We stood there for a few minutes, letting that bit of depressing sentiment hang in the air. Life generally sucks most of the time. I awkwardly shuffled my weight back and forth.

Bullard finally broke the stalemate. "You need a ride?"

"Nah, I'm good. My car is parked around here somewhere." I hooked a finger over my shoulder. "I'm gonna head home and sleep this off."

"Alright, Halson, see you tomorrow."

"Not if I see you first," I called back as I walked away. I didn't have to turn around to know there was a disgruntled look on his face. His life would be a lot more boring if I wasn't around to wreak havoc and get into trouble.

He should really thank me, I thought as I walked through the parking lot.

Where the hell was my car, anyways?

Chapter 9

I was strapped to a chair by a short, fat, toad-like woman in a nurse's outfit. The room was black except for one of those big round surgery lights that hung above the table. It didn't shed much light, only encompassing the table and a few feet beyond. In the dark, where the light couldn't reach, things stirred and moved. They didn't dare enter the circle of light, so they waited, hungry, and watched.

The nurse tied a rubber strap around my arm so the veins bulged beneath the skin. She then opened her mouth, and instead of teeth, there were rows of sharp metal needles. The wide maw opened even further as she began to emit a high-pitched wailing noise. The nurse's head swung forward, burying its needle teeth into my flesh.

I woke up screaming to my phone ringing for attention. Cold sweat covered my body as the remnants of the dream began to fade away. I looked at the clock, and it was early in the morning.

Normally, a call this early would be an annoyance to people, but I was grateful to have been torn out of my nightmare.

I picked up the phone and gave a half hearten grumble of hello.

"Hey, boss, you there?"

It was Anita. I wondered what she was calling about so early in the morning. It had been nearly a week since starting the case, and almost every night, my sleep had been plagued with the wrong kinds of naughty nurse dreams.

Being awake was not much of an improvement. Since that first day, I hadn't made any more progress. I had been stuck in *Groundhog Day*, an endless cycle of office workers and white-collar drones either giving me the cold shoulder or telling me they were too busy. I'd been hoping to hit another gold mine of information, but none of the people I managed to pin down had been Chatty Cathys. The police were busy running the blood drive angle, so I hadn't heard a peep out of Bullard or Benson. I was a little annoyed they had all but cut me out of the loop while hanging my ass out as bait. It made me feel a little better to pad out the invoice I was gonna send them. It was a small consolation I was gonna make out on this job, but my landlord would probably be happy I might be able to pay off some of my back rent.

"What's up?" I mumbled into the phone.

"We got a problem down here at the office."

"What kind of problem? The toilet is backing up again kind of problem or annoyed customer/landlord looking for me kind of problem?" I looked at my alarm clock through blurry vision. The alarm hadn't worked since the time I pistol-whipped it to shut up that annoying beeping.

"The police are here kind of trouble."

That made me sit up, my mind racing with all kinds of situations that would result in the police showing up at my office, none of them good.

"What's going on?" I struggled to pull my pants on while juggling the phone against my ear. I nearly tripped and almost fell on my head.

"You have to see for yourself."

"I'll be right there." I grabbed my keys as I headed to the car, leaving the handset dangling off the hook.

I arrived at my office in record time. I may or may not have blown through a red light or two on my way across town. The drive had been a blur as my mind raced, coming up with all kinds of horrible things that could've happened. It was a little anticlimactic when I finally parked. I was forced to get out down the street from my office as the area in front was blocked by a black and white.

"Looks like someone was out having some fun last night," Anita said as we stood on the sidewalk outside the office.

Shards of glass were littered all around us. Every single window in the building had been broken. Sunlight glittered off the shards, the effect quite pretty in the morning sun.

"Was anyone hurt?" I asked.

I'd noticed no other building on the street had suffered any damage. It didn't exclusively mean that this was a personal attack on us. The shooter could've been a person who was displeased with the plumbing company on the first floor. I know having to stare at a plumber's crack tends to make me feel a little homicidal.

"Nah, seems it was done late at night when no one was around. I called the cops when I came in and saw it this morning." Anita was disturbingly unphased by this.

Our office was not in the best neighborhood, but it wasn't the projects where people shoot out streetlights. While it was the best I could afford, at least we didn't have gangbangers hanging out on the corners or anything. A drive-by was out of character for our area. My office had been here for three years, and we'd never had so much as a vandalism. Okay, maybe a little graffiti, but that was kid stuff.

"Well, let's hope they were pissed 'bout a poorly fixed toilet. Any damage to the office?"

"Doesn't look like it. Pretty much just the front windows and some holes in the hallway walls."

I nodded as she told me. It sounded like someone with a small-caliber handgun. Had they been serious and using an automatic rifle, they would've Swiss-cheesed the hell out of the front of the building.

The uniformed officer was standing in the open door of his cruiser, talking on the radio. Other than Anita and myself, we were the only people on the street.

It was smart. No one wanted to be drawn into this mess. It's funny how it reflected human nature the same way when dealing with the supernatural. Not their problem. If they don't see it, then it doesn't exist, and they can keep pretending everything's fine. Living in a constant state of denial as the darkness lurked all around them. At times, I pitied those with their heads buried in the sand, and at others, I believed they deserved it when they got bit in the ass.

An unmarked car turned onto the street and slowly made its way toward us. It pulled short of the barricade the cop had put up in the street, and Alex got out. She ran a hand through her blonde hair as she closed the door, causing it to catch and reflect the sunlight in the same way the shards of glass did. She sashayed her way across the road and toward us.

She wore skinny jeans that looked molded to her body. Even though it was already heating up, she still had a black leather jacket on over a black t-shirt, probably to hide her gun. Her motorcycle boots clicked loudly with each step. I could hear them clearly even from my distance. She didn't really look like a cop at all. She looked like almost any other woman in any other setting. It was her eyes that didn't fit. They were narrowed in concentration and focused on one thing: me. *Oh boy.*

"Uh oh, here comes trouble," said Anita. "I'm gonna go see about getting someone out here to replace these widows. See ya, lover boy."

Before I could even object, she'd scooted through the front door and disappeared into the building, leaving me to weather the brunt of the storm that was coming. I braced for impact.

"What did you do this time, Halson?" Alex scowled at me, just assuming I'm always the cause of trouble. Which is unfair, since trouble just kinda follows me. I swear, I'm not the cause. Usually, sometimes...okay, I'm pretty sure there *are* times when it's not my fault. Like this one.

"Not me, but some jerk was joy riding last night." I growled.

"This far south? Seems unusual. Not unexpected, just—"

"Yeah, I know, but if I jumped at every shadow, I wouldn't get anything done, and people would think I was paranoid."

"Just because you're paranoid doesn't mean there aren't people out to get you. You've pissed a lot of people, Halson." Alex sighed. "I wouldn't be shocked if there was a line for people wanting to kill you."

"Me?" I said, playing as innocent as I could muster. "Who would want to kill little ole me? I'm as innocent as a lamb."

She snorted in laughter. "I dunno, but I'm pretty sure the line starts behind me."

Her smile was pretty. I still don't know what would give anyone the idea we would work together. For all of her hard edge, no-nonsense, put-up job, she was still too naive.

"So, what brings Philly's finest out to my lowly neighborhood? I can't believe they'd call you out for something like this.

Heck, we barely rate one patrolman." I leaned back against the building. The sun was hardly up, and I could already tell today was gonna be a scorcher. "I haven't heard so much as a peep out of you guys in the last week."

"We've been following up on the blood donation link. Lots of red tape and dead ends. We managed to match the gauge marks on Baker's neck to that of an extraction pump found in the clinic. Normally, those pumps are used in morgues to drain the blood from a bod. Funeral homes use them to embalm bodies. Outside of that, mainly we've been looking for the nurse who was stationed at the B&B building. It's been pretty much a wild goose chase since no one had seen her since the day before Baker was killed. Until early this morning, a janitor found this." She reached into her jacket and pulled out a picture.

I took it when she handed it to me and looked at it. It was a close-up shot of a severed arm. It had been torn off about halfway up the forearm. The slim wrist and manicured nails gave it away as clearly belonging to a female. The stump was shredded, and the bones were visible just beyond it. I also noticed there was very little blood. When a limb is severed, the arteries gush blood everywhere, which meant the lady had been dead when she'd lost the arm, or she'd died in another place and, while moving the body, the limb came off.

"Got any shots from a farther away angle?" I wanted to see more of the scene to check my theory.

Alex handed me three more photos. The first was a bit further back, showing the arm lying on a dirty cement floor. There were no signs of blood, but it was still too close to tell. The second was much farther away, showing the whole scene. The room was more the subject of this photo. It was bare concrete with a couple of conduits running up the wall. There was light, but it was dimmer than what most common areas. Almost like a basement room, but not quite.

I couldn't place my finger on it, but it seemed familiar. I wracked my mind trying to place it, but it was too early, and my brain just didn't want to cooperate.

Finally, it clicked, and I recognized the stairwell as the one leading to the basement of the B&B building. I was surprised it had taken me so long, considering I'd spent quite a bit of time over the last week skulking in their stairways, trying to catch some less than reputable employees sneaking a smoke. That turned out to be a dry well. I guess kids who played hooky in school don't grow up to get white-collar jobs in investment firms.

"See anything we missed?"

"Yeah, your victim was killed somewhere else, and the killer dropped the limb while carrying the body out of the building." I was winging it, but managed to make it sound nonchalant enough to cover that fact.

"We kind of figured that out from the lack of blood, Halson. We aren't amateurs. Despite what you'd like to think of us, most cops are actually pretty good at their jobs."

"Really? Are these the same people who think it's a vampire attack? Cause last time I checked, vampires don't use tools." I held up one of the pictures.

"What are you talking about?" Alex took the photo from me.

"If you look at the bone, you can see gouge marks. Those are caused by a tool by someone who isn't used to cutting through bone. Joints are much easier to cut than the bone itself, and this one is cut through the thickest, hardest part of the forearm."

I was lying. It took one glance for me to recognize what it really was. Those marks weren't caused by any tool, but by something with sharp teeth gnawing through the bone as if it were a breadstick. Not something a human could do. I just hoped Alex was enough of a city kid to not see through my bullshit.

"Well shit," she said. "I don't know how CSI could've missed this."

"I believe you were saying something about cops being good at their jobs?" I mocked.

"Say one more word, Halson, and I will bounce your head off that brick wall."

I didn't say a word. I just gave her another of my shit-eating grins. God, pushing her buttons was just too much fun.

She was so pissed that she had to take a few deep breaths. She stood with her hands on her hips, looking at her feet while she gathered herself. She was kinda cute when she was angry. Less so when she was taking that anger out on me. So, I let her be and didn't interrupt her.

Once she'd pulled herself back from the edge of homicidal rage, she let out a sigh. "Okay, Halson, I got to get back to the office and follow up on this. Try not to do anything stupid in the meantime, alright?"

"I don't have to try," I said.

That made her let out a bark of laughter, and she just shook her head as she walked away.

I watched her go, waiting until she was out of sight before I rushed back to my car. The office troubles would have to wait. I wanted to check out my hunch while there was still plenty of daylight outside. I was hoping I was wrong, and that it would turn out to be nothing, but if I was right, things were about to get a whole lot messier.

The Road Runner's engine roared as I fired her up and headed back downtown.

Chapter 10

I slunk back into the B&B building through a rear entrance the janitors had left propped open with a bucket. I'd been using it to come and go unseen for most of the past week after becoming chummy with the cleaning crew. They were a hell of a lot nicer than the main staff or even the office employees. Being downtrodden and treated as crap gave them the same disdain for the suit-wearing stiffs I had. Plus, once they saw how fancy office workers looked down their noses at me, they saw me as a kindred spirit. It also didn't hurt I'd played myself off as a plain old working Joe like them with a brutish boss breathing down my neck. While it wasn't exactly true, it also wasn't far from the truth.

They were a nice enough bunch to let me go about as I pleased without alerting the building security. Not that I wasn't allowed to be there. I was technically part of the ongoing police investigation, but I didn't really need or want the hassle, especially not after having tangled with that one security guard twice and getting him fired. I doubted his coworkers would've been too happy to put up with me, or maybe not. From what gossip I'd gotten from the cleaning and maintenance staff, he hadn't been well-liked. Which I guess was good for me. They were a great source of information on gossip. However, not much help beyond that, and no one really knew much about what was happening on the top floors. It seemed to me like the higher up you went, the less was known, and the more tight-lipped people were.

Right now, I wasn't interested in the upper floors. I was headed in the other direction. In the stairwell, instead of climbing up the countless flights of stairs, I headed down. The maintenance tunnels and boiler room were located in the basement of the building, and no one went there alone. One of the Hispanic maintenance guys had told me people hated going down there. Strange noises, he'd said. Strange noises and the feeling of being watched. When I asked how long this had been going on, he'd said just in the past few weeks.

What most people chalk up to a gut feeling or as sixth sense are the remnants of our primal animal instincts. When it feels like someone or something is watching you, it's usually because something is. You just can't see it. Though they don't know it, they're instinctively detecting the presence of a preternatural creature. In school as kids, we're taught there are just five senses, but in truth, there are dozens, possibly hundreds, of senses science just hasn't named yet. I'd read an article once that said there were twenty-eight different identifiable senses scientists knew of, and those are what people mistake for a "sixth" sense. We're unaware of it, but those old senses are still looking out for us.

I hadn't paid the stories any attention at the time because, well, that's the kinda shit that pops up everywhere, and to be honest, it's a sane reaction to creepy places. Mainly, I'd dismissed it because my attention had been focused on the upper floors, which had been stupid of me to discount and fly in the face of all my training. I had ignored something that had been right under my nose.

I crept down the stairs, trying to find the spot that matched the photos. I hadn't thought to palm one of them when I'd handed them back to Alex, and now I was kicking myself over it. My memory isn't exactly the best or most reliable at times, and given how often I'd taken blows to the head, it was probably a miracle I didn't have brain damage. Or maybe I did. All the monsters were just in my head, and I was in an institute somewhere wearing a straitjacket in a padded room.

I managed to find a spot that more or less looked like the one in the photos. I backed up and held up my hands, trying to frame it like in the photograph. When I was pretty sure I was in the right place, I looked around for signs of anything unusual.

It was evident pretty quickly I was gonna find nothing. The alcove was as clean as such places ever get. No trash, no marks or indicators of any kind of struggle. No convenient scrap of paper or matchbook telling me who the killer was or where the rest of the body was. Either the police had done too good of a job cleaning up after themselves, or there was nothing here to find. That left me with only one option left. I was going to have to extend my search to the creepy ass basement to look for clues...all by myself.

Lucky me.

I heaved open the heavy basement door. It wasn't easy since it wasn't really meant for people to go in and out, which made sense. It also helped to block out the noise. Maintenance areas are pretty noisy. Not loud, just noisy. Water pipes, steam pipes, and various electrical equipment all humming and rattling, putting out heat and clatter.

The heavy door closed behind me with a *bang*, seriously cutting the amount of light. It wasn't dark in the tunnels, and that's what they felt like: tunnels. They were lit with those low-cost utility lights. Areas like this didn't need much illumination as they were just supposed to do their jobs to pump out climate control and electricity for the floors above.

I felt like, at any moment, I would come across some Morlocks, toiling away, thinking of eating the Eloi on the floors above.

The thought sent shivers down my spine. I was scaring myself for no reason, or so I tried to tell myself. Unfortunately, I wasn't buying it. The scar that ran the length of my spine was a reminder it wasn't so easy to dismiss, especially at times like this. It was a constant reminder that monsters were all too real.

I unholstered my 1911, and the weight of the .45 was comforting. I always found it reassuring when I held my dad's gun in my hand. It was almost as if he were here with me, telling me not to be afraid.

I made my way slowly through the tunnels, letting the gun lead the way. Anything that surprised me was going to have a very bad day. I just hoped it wasn't some hapless janitor doing his job.

I'd almost convinced myself I was wasting my time and I should just turn around to hustle my dumbass back to the exit. Then, I picked up the smell. There were plenty down here: grease, mold, damp. It all mixed to create a musty atmosphere. At first, I figured I was picking up on the metallic from the pipes, but there was coppery taste on my tongue with a rotten aftertaste.

The smell of blood, and a lot of it. The further I went, the stronger it got. The last corner I turned, it hit me like a truck. The oppressive scent of something dead. It was mixed with another more powerful odor, like burning socks and rotten eggs. I spit on the ground, the saliva in my mouth greasy and foul, the smell was so strong.

I hunkered down and walked in a crouch as I began to hear noises. I focused my attention in the direction ahead of me, narrowing my hearing in that area and concentrating on the sounds. They were wet with sharp crunching.

My stomach did a slow flip as I reconfigured what those sounds were, and I didn't want to be right. They were the sounds of something eating, and I could only think of a few things that were wet and crunchy at the same time, none of them good. When I reached the next corner, I paused, hoping it was just someone eating celery with a mouthful of peanut butter.

Peeking around the corner, I noted the space beyond opened into a sort of hub. Pipes met and nestled less than a foot from the ceiling. Conduits running from the various tunnels converged and diverged on to other places. The other side of the room, maybe fifty feet or so, ended in a wall covered in electrical boxes and breakers. Sitting in one corner was a large boxy piece of equipment, a furnace or air conditioner. I didn't know enough to tell which. The place looked exactly like you would expect a maintenance room to look like in one of the factory scenes where dumb teens get murdered by Freddy Krueger.

What was in the middle of the room was far, far worse.

It was hunched over nearly double on the floor, knobby knees sticking up higher than its head as its pale skin seemed to glow in the dim orange running lights. The creature was emaciated to the point it was little more than a skeleton with papery skin. It extremely skinny limbs only served to make them look longer and more skeletal. Its ribcage was visible through its chest, and I could count every single vertebra in its back from where I was hiding. Its head was little more than a skull with minimal human features. Its ears were long and pointed, and its eyes were deep black pits with glowing red embers in its sockets.

Eyes I saw every night in my dreams.

Inhumanly long fingers, sporting dinosaur-like claws stained black with blood, held the carcass of what I could only guess to be a rat to its mouth. Like the hands, its mouth was also streaked with blood as the creature tore at the remains of its meal. Its teeth were rat-like with the front two being long and sharp. Its nose and chin were sloped and pointed, giving the face a pinched, rodent-ish appearance.

If you've ever seen the old black-and-white *Dracula* movie, you know exactly what this creature was. Nosferatu. Dangerous, feral vampires, who were more animal-like than what people typically think of vampires. These were to regular vampires what crack addicts are to accountants. Despite their frail appearance, they are insanely fast, agile, and strong. They were living, breathing murder machines with only one thought in their deformed, hideous skulls: kill.

Even experienced hunters avoid Nosferatu when they can. They make hunting the kinds of vampires I usually kill look like harmless babies. To give you an example of how deadly a Nosferatu attack is—it would be less deadly to shove your face into a running lawnmower blade.

Not only was this thing uber dangerous, but I also wasn't packing even my regular hunting gear, much less what would be needed to take this thing down. I had my old Colt handgun. That meant I had seven in the mag, one in the chamber, and a spare backup mag for a total of sixteen rounds. Which wasn't going to tickle that thing, much less put it down. I would have to retreat and come back when better prepared. Like with a tank or a bomb. A big bomb that would drop the whole building on it.

I was easing my way back from the corner when there was a sound behind me. I spun with lighting speed, operating entirely on reflex. Before my brain could catch up, I was already in a combat crouch, two-handing my gun and leveling it at…Captain Bullard?

I blinked, confused. I'd been so focused on the Nosferatu, I hadn't heard him sneak up on me. That probably hadn't been hard for the big man with all the background noise. You didn't exactly need to be a ninja to sneak up on a distracted person down here. I was more confounded by how he knew I was here.

My consternation didn't last long as Alex stepped out from behind him. I knew instantly she had played me. She hadn't fallen for my lie. She'd let me think she had so I would run off and lead her in the right direction. Once I'd left, she'd doubled back and snitched on me to Bullard. Then they met up and followed me here without realizing the danger they were putting us all in.

Idiots.

Alex was naïve and didn't realize how dangerous my job was, but Bullard knew better. He'd seen me in the field firsthand, and knew vampires were not something you took lightly. Hell, it was the whole reason Bullard even let me operate accosted. Why did he pick now, of all times, to not trust me?

They were both wearing flak jackets with PSIC emblazoned in big yellow letters. Bullard had his riot gun leveled at my chest. The shotgun looked small in his big hands. Alex was two-handing her police-issue Glock, clearly knowing how to handle the firearm. They looked like they were getting ready to raid a local drug den. It wasn't enough to deal with a vampire, much less the horror they didn't know was lurking around the corner. I furiously tried to wave them back, but they ignored me and moved closer.

"See, I told you he was lying to cut us out," Alex hissed in a low voice.

I slammed my finger to my lips, angrily signaling her to shut the fuck up.

She clearly did not get the message.

"What's going on here, Halson? You'd better have a goddamn good explanation." Bullard lifted the shotgun, aiming over my head, scanning the corridor for threats.

"For the love of God, get the hell out of here," I hissed at them, trying to keep my voice down as much as possible. At least they had the sense to whisper. "You two fucking idiots have no clue how much danger we're all in right now. We must get out of here before it notices us."

"What notices us?" Alex's voice got a little louder than it should've been in her anger.

I whipped my head back to peer around the corner. My blood ran cold. It was gone. The spot where the Nosferatu had been crouched was now empty. My gaze darted around, searching every nook, cranny, and corner trying to spot it. It was nowhere to be seen. That was not good.

I turned back to the cops. "*Run!*" I growled. "We need to be back to the exit as quickly as possible. It knows we're here."

"Wait, what knows we're here?" Alex asked, confused at the shift in my tone from anger to fear.

Bullard saw the look on my face and how serious this had become. He grabbed Alex's shoulder with one big hand and spun her around, giving her a shove back the way they came.

"Go. Now." He wasted no words. He just moved his subordinate at a pace quick enough to allow them to still cover themselves, but not linger any longer than absolutely necessary.

I didn't have time to explain exactly what we were up against. Our only hope now was to make it out before it found us. I followed close behind as we quickly fell into a coordinated team, keeping our eyes open and our corners covered. Hope was starting to creep into my mind, that maybe it had run off because it didn't know exactly where we were. Maybe, just maybe, we would make it out and get away Scott-free.

Hope is a sucker's game for a reason. Just when you think you're safe, reality, that heartless bitch, pulls the rug out from under you.

"Halson, what's down here?" Alex called back to me.

I didn't get a chance to answer as that was the exact moment it hit us. It moved so fast, it was little more than a pale blur.

Alex was thrown to the ground from the impact. The front of her vest ripped to shreds. The Kevlar had been shredded like paper, but it managed to protect her from the monster's claws. It wouldn't survive another hit. The vest was basically useless now.

I tried to track the Nosferatu's movements, but it ricocheted like a pinball back up among the pipes where I lost it.

It was using the pipes along the ceiling to move around, dropping down to ambush its prey with its speed. It wasn't just fast and strong, this one was smart and had already devised a pretty nasty hunting strategy. We would have a hard time seeing it among the pipes. With its thin limbs and pale skin, it blended in too well. Our only hope was to keep moving.

Bullard scooped Alex up and put her back on her feet. The young woman probably weighed nothing to the big man, but that wasn't the biggest problem. The attack had been so fast and viscous, it had left her a bit shell-shocked. She seemed confused and unaware of where she was. Bullard shouldered her behind him and took up the lead, keeping her between the two of us.

As we started moving, I got lucky and spotted the creature hiding among some ceiling pipes, stalking us, preparing for another sneak attack. I sent a round in its direction, and it dove out of sight.

Alex whipped around at the discharge, catching the tail end of the vampire vanishing.

"What the hell is that thing, Halson?"

"Keep moving!" I yelled and fired another bullet in that direction, trying to keep it at bay. I didn't even have time to explain to them the trouble we were in. I just had to keep us moving towards the exit.

Bullard pulled up short, and Alex and I nearly ran into him.

I looked around his tank of a back to see what had caused him to stop. At the end of the corridor, low to the ground, I saw it peeking out. The Nosferatu had circled around to ambush us as we rounded the corner, but Bullard had spotted it before we got too close. It slowly slunk out from around the corner, low to the ground, in a completely inhuman way. Its eyes burned with murder, and it hissed at us, its lips drawing back from long yellow rat teeth.

The captain didn't bat an eye. He just hauled off and blasted the creature. It nimbly dodged the blast, buckshot smashing holes in the cement wall behind it the size of fists. The vampire clung to the ceiling and skittered towards us like a giant spider. Bullard pumped round after round at it, but it kept ducking out of the way with lighting speed. When the shotgun ran dry, he stepped back and took a knee to reload.

Alex, with most of her wits back together, stepped in front of him, taking a firing stance, and opened fire on the approaching horror. Their coordination was seamless. The kind you only get from hours of training and trust between partners. I tried to cover them the best I could from the rear.

Alex's little Glock fared no better as the monster closed the distance and just started to wade through the hail of gunfire. The 9mm carried a lot less power than a scatter gun, so when she managed to hit it, the Nosferatu didn't even seem to notice. It dropped from the ceiling and landed on her like a brick house. It buried her under its wiry body. All I could make out were her thrashing legs as it lowered its head towards her neck.

I couldn't risk shooting it. The body was too thin, and I could just as easily hit Alex, so I threw myself at its bony back. Since I couldn't shoot, I used the butt of the heavy .45 to club it about its head and shoulders as I tried to pull it off her.

Alex had managed to get her arms up to protect herself, but they did little good against the titanic strength of the monster astride her. She hadn't been able to throw it off, but when it had gone for her throat, she'd been able to turn her body just enough that its jaws had fastened on the thick shoulder strap of her bullet-proof vest. The creature harried at the Kevlar like a dog with a bone, having a tougher time tearing through it than flesh. But it wouldn't hold long. The seams popped as the fabric that could stop bullets began to tear as though it was a cheap cotton t-shirt.

The creature eventually registered my annoying pounding and swatted me like the fly I might as well have been. The rail-thin arm was like a steel rod and hit me with enough force to send me flying off, crashing into a nearby wall. I hit with a dull thud like a sack of wet laundry, and slid down to the floor. The impact had knocked the air out of me, and I sat there dazed for a second.

Once I had shaken the cobwebs from my brain and regained my ability to breathe, I noticed Bullard had taken my position on the thing's back. He'd gotten his shotgun around the creature's neck. He must've figured he couldn't use it any more than I could've used my handgun, and was exhausting leverage to pull the animal off Alex in a Full Nelson.

Its jaws snapped angrily as it tried to throw the big man off, but he hung on like a bull rider. Each time it twisted or bucked, he moved with it, keeping his grip and balance. He couldn't match the creature in pure strength, but he knew how to use what he had to his advantage. It made me wonder just how many fights Bullard had been in growing up. Wrestling was good exercise, but it's no use in a real fight. To use a move like that in a real life-or-death fight takes skill and tons of experience. It also probably meant he had grown up fighting guys a lot bigger and stronger than him.

That's when things went wrong. Hard to believe, I know, but being chased and attacked by a murder machine we didn't stand a chance against sounds bad, but things can always be worse. That lesson I learned on a weekly basis.

Alex scrambled to her feet, but was too close to the grappling pair, and the Nosferatu managed to catch her with a vicious backhand to the mouth. Her body instantly went boneless, and her head rolled as though her neck was broken while blood gushed from her mouth. She hit the floor, sprawled like a puppet with its strings cut.

It caused a split-second lapse in Bullard's concentration, and he wasn't ready when the Nosferatu thrust its hips back as it jerked forward, throwing the easily two-hundred-and-fifty-pound man over its shoulders as if he weighed nothing.

We nearly crashed into each other as I dove to try to reach Alex. I swear, the whole building shook when he landed, and I barely avoided being caught beneath him.

If it had knocked the wind out of him, Bullard didn't show it. He was back up on his knees and spun to face the creature. That was the wrong move, or better to say, there were no right moves. Once he'd lost his grip and the vampire threw him, it was over. His quick recovery only meant he saw it coming when the vampire killed him.

The Nosferatu struck like a snake, fastening its jaws around the man's throat. There was a horrible crunching as it bit down, and blood sprayed from the now-severed arteries.

Bullard made one last wet gurgling sound as the life was ripped out of him. The vampire viciously twisted its head and tore his throat out, leaving a bloody, jagged hole where it had been. Blood cascaded down the front of his vest, looking very black in the poor lighting of the basement.

Bullard was a good man and didn't deserve this. He deserved better than dying in some dirty basement beneath a corporate monument to how cheap human life was. Another good person had died trying to save my stupid life.

It wasn't fair. So many good, decent people had died while I kept on living. They say you can't put a value on human life, no matter how much people try. But even an idiot like me knows the truly good people like Bullard, who put their life on the line every day and believe in real justice, equality, and all that shit, are worth more than my dumbass. By comparison, I wasn't worth two squirts of piss, yet here, again, was another life added to an already steep debt I could never repay in a thousand lifetimes. He had a family, a wife, and a son who would never get to see him alive again. Another family destroyed by these monsters, and they wouldn't stop until they were wiped off the face of the earth.

My anger boiled over, and I reacted on pure instinct. I dove for the dropped shotgun.

The sudden movement attracted the Nosferatu's attention. It had been licking up the spilled blood and turned its attention to its new perceived threat. My hands had barely touched the weapon before it leapt.

I rolled, bringing the shotgun to bare as I landed on my back just as the vampire came down on me. I thrust the barrel at its face as its fangs bared. It caught the barrel between its teeth, and I pulled the trigger.

Time slowed down to a crawl. The thing's eyes bulged in surprise as the shotgun erupted in its mouth. Its cheeks puffed out, cartoon-like, before they exploded in plumes of fire and burning propellant that engulfed its face and head.

I held the trigger down and worked the pump rapidly, slam-firing the gun until everything above the lower jaw disappeared into a red mist.

The creature let out a choking gurgle and toppled over backward. I pushed myself up from the floor, unsatisfied. I wanted more. I wanted it to hurt and suffer for what it did. I wanted to burn it with my anger until nothing was left but scorched earth and ash. I wanted the whole world to feel the same pain and injustice.

I stepped over the Nosferatu's body. I had one shell left. I racked the pump, chambering the round. I put the muzzle against the thing's chest, just above its heart, and pulled the trigger. I blew its heart to a pulp. All that remained was a hole clean through its chest. I could even see where its spine had nearly snapped in half. It wasn't dead, but it would do until I burned the rest of it to ash.

Right now, I had other things to worry about. I had to check to see if Alex was still alive and, if so, how badly she was hurt.

She had gotten lucky. The hit she'd taken had just knocked her senseless. Her eyes were half-open, but weren't focused, and she wasn't coherent. The worst of it seemed to be a badly busted lip. It had split open the left side of her upper lip pretty badly, and like all head wounds, it looked worse than it was due to all the blood.

I managed to roll her over my shoulders in a fireman's carry. She was a lot heavier than she looked. Of course, she was limp, so it was all dead weight. The hard part was getting the exit door open. It had been substantial without an injured woman draped over my back. I managed to get it open by pummeling it with my head and feet. Then, it was slow getting up the stairs as I was a little dizzy from smacking my head against the metal maintenance door.

Once out on the curb, I used her car radio to call in emergency services.

The response was quick. Cops don't mess around when it comes to losing one of their own. Squad cars and an ambulance were on the scene in less than five minutes.

In that time, Alex had more or less regained consciousness, though she was still a bit loopy. I turned her over to the paramedics, but she refused to go to the hospital. I left them to tend to her wounds and addressing her lip, leading the recovery squad to the basement.

The scene was worse now that the danger was over. Bullard's body seemed smaller somehow, as though whatever made him who he was seemed to magnify his size. His personality was so big that his body stretched to fit it. Now, it was just an empty shell, a lump of meat, no different than any other.

My heart was so heavy, and it sank as I watched the coroners zip him up in a body bag. It hadn't dawned on me how much I considered the man a friend until that moment, and I wanted to cry, but tough vampire hunters don't cry, at least, not where people can see. It felt like I was nine-years-old again when I'd lost my family. I hadn't cried then. I'd just felt a white-hot ball of rage in the pit of my stomach.

Nothing had changed in almost twenty years. Someone else had died because I'd been too weak to stop it. I'd stood by and watched as the monsters took another person from me.

The Nosferatu's body had gone ashy gray, and as it withered, the contractions of its dry muscles had curled it into a ball. Headless and with a gaping hole in its chest, it looked hardly any bigger than a child. It was almost unbelievable that, not even an hour ago, it had been one of the deadliest, most powerful creatures on earth.

I had gotten lucky, and this was the only reason Alex and I were still alive. That was the story of my life when it came down to it. I survived on sheer dumb luck while those around me died in my place. When I was younger, I used to think I was cursed, but now I know *I* was the curse. That's why it had to be me and no one else who killed these monsters.

I made a mental note to pay a visit to the coroner's office later to dispose of the vampire's body. It was about as dead as they could get, but there was always a chance that, given enough time, they could regenerate, even from that level of damage. But it could wait a day or two. It wasn't like I could just walk off with it with all these cops around. If Bullard had been in charge, it would've been different, but he would never be in charge again. I would have to settle for a little B&E.

The scene cleared pretty quickly. No one wanted to hang around in a creepy basement, especially where a fellow officer had met his end. It was bad juju, and no one wanted to linger. From start to finish, the whole thing lasted less than two hours. Now, it was just police tape and chalk outlines. Oh, and one crest-fallen idiot who had walked everyone into this mess. It had been hell waiting for the CSI guys, but it had been better than going upstairs and telling Alex her partner was dead. I know I was a coward for letting someone else do it, but what more could you really expect from me? Plus, I don't really do well with that emotional support part of people. Another casualty of my lifestyle.

Once I was alone, I backtracked to the spot where I'd first found the Nosferatu. The open room was about the widest and most open area down here, and that didn't really make sense.

First off, how did it get in? While they may have started as humans, Nosferatu aren't much smarter than animals. Whatever turns them into those things instead of typical vampires seems to rob them of any real higher intelligence. So, it's not like it just wandered in, given the number of doors and stairs between there and outside. It wasn't practical, and such an open space made a pretty unappealing lair. They have animal intelligence, and so they do animal-like behavior. They would make a nest or lair in a more secluded spot. They avoid populated areas unless hunting.

Someone locked it in here, and whoever it was must've been trying to throw us off the trail. They give the PSIC unit their vampire and hope they wrap it all up nice and neat, then go away.

Unfortunately for them, it wasn't just the cops. I was on the case, too, and I've been told on more than one occasion I'm like a pitbull with a soup bone. Once I've set my teeth into something, I don't let it go, and now that blood had been spilled, it was personal.

I didn't care who or what was behind all of this, but I was going to make them pay.

Normally when I killed, I did so with cold professional detachment. This time, I was going to take pleasure in watching the light go out of their eyes.

Chapter 11

I got back to the ambulance just in time to find Alex threatening to shoot an EMT who was trying to bundle her away in the back. Intervening, I saved the poor guy's life and talked her into letting me take her home. The EMT gave Alex some drugs for her split lip, recommending she see a doctor as soon as she could.

With that, I got her into a cab and back to her place.

Alex's apartment was nice. It was in Washington Square, an upscale neighborhood. Not the most affluent, but way better than anything I could afford. It didn't help that her apartment was a third-floor walkup in a brownstone. While she didn't weigh much, Alex had one of those deceptively slim, athletic builds, and I usually wouldn't have had a hard time getting her up three flights of stairs, but after the stress of the attack and the adrenaline worn off, I was exhausted. I was running on fumes, and just wanted to crawl into bed and sleep for the rest of the year. This was a deep in your bones tired.

Somehow, I managed to get the two of us into her place and plopped her onto the couch. I collapsed next to her, needing desperately to rest.

I could not have been more out of place. Her décor was done up Danish-modern. Everything was too neat and clean. Everything had its place, and the room was so orderly, it was like it was put together with the attention of a psychopath. It felt wrong. Sterile. Like it was all staged. Like Alex didn't spend much time here, and she was so married to the job, she had no home life. Her place reflected the housekeeper more than it did her.

"Hey, Halson." Her voice was thin and strained.

She was curled up on her side next to me, her head under her arms. The hood of the sweatshirt she'd borrowed was pulled up to hide her face. I knew it was to mask her tears. With all of the stress and trauma she'd witnessed, she was an emotional wreck. You have to build up resistance to it, and the only way to do that is with repeated exposure. God knows, I didn't want that for her. It would be weeks, if not months, of therapy before she would be anything approaching fine. That's only if she took the rational, normal person route. From the look of her apartment, she would undoubtedly throw herself into her work until she had a meltdown. Something I was all too familiar with.

"Halson." Her voice was steadier as she started again. "Thanks for everything. If you hadn't...I mean, that thing. That thing, it was so fast. It came out of nowhere, and it...it killed Darren. It would have killed me, too, if you hadn't been there."

"It's not your fault," I replied.

"I know it's not my fault!" She exploded.

"No, I don't mean that. I mean, it's my fault. I lied to you. I didn't want you guys to get involved." I hung my head. "If I had warned you, then maybe you wouldn't have gone in. Or we could've planned something. Stupid, stupid. I'm such an idiot."

"It's not your fault, either, Halson. It's that monster's fault. It's the fault of the asshole who killed Baker and started all this." She sat up, her eyes burning furiously. "We'll make it right by finding that asshole and nailing him to the wall. That's what we'll do."

She looked beautiful in her anger. It made her resemble a vengeful Valkyrie, ready to storm onto the battlefield, looking for a glorious death.

"No, what you have to do is rest, and get your bearings back."

"No, I'll tell you what I need, Halson."

Before I knew what was happening, she threw one leg over me and straddled my lap. All I could do was look into those startling blue eyes as she leaned in and kissed me, ignoring her freshly split and stitched lip. It was full and passionate, and her lips tasted sweet with a slight hint of blood.

She abruptly broke the kiss, and before I could protest, she'd pulled the sweatshirt up over her head, leaving her bare from the waist up.

Oh God, all that smooth, pale skin was a hell of a sight. Her breasts were firm and full. She took my hands and guided them along her hips, up across her tight stomach, and eventually to cup her breasts gently in my palms as she kissed me again.

I was suddenly no longer tired. I was wired, like I had just downed a dozen shots of espresso, and I could've run a marathon. Everything below my waist was reporting on all systems go, and the rocket was ready to launch. She was so warm, soft, and beautiful, and she was right here with her motor running and wanting it.

I closed my eyes and made a Herculean effort that should've gotten my man card revoked.

"Alex, we can't." I gently but firmly eased her off me and back onto the couch as I stood up. I needed to put distance between us while I still had self-control.

"What? Why not, Halson? We've been going at it practically since the moment we met. Why not *really* go at it? We're both adults, it's fine."

"No, it's not. It would be taking advantage of you."

"How are you taking advantage of me? I'm telling you it's okay and it's what I want."

"You're not in your right mind."

"How am I not in my right mind? I'm saying yes, Halson. What kind of man turns down sex?"

"You're all ramped up from the stress and what happened. Your hormones are out of whack, and you aren't thinking straight. All the death has got you overcompensating. And I can't take advantage of you like this."

She looked at me aghast. Her ears turned red, and she became self-conscious, concealing her breasts behind her hands. "I'm not some sort of frail little girl. I can handle myself. I don't need you treating me like I'm some PTSD-addled victim."

"I'm speaking from experience. A shock like that makes you act in ways you wouldn't if you were in your right mind," I explained. "And I'm not going to take advantage of you in this state."

"Oh, so you're too nice of a guy to sleep with me because you think my judgment is compromised?" She rolled her eyes as she ran her hands through her hair. "What a white knight you are, Halson."

I ignored that. I knew she was just speaking out of hurt and frustration. She was running hot and looking for something, or anything, to take the edge off to try to forget about it for a while. I had done the same thing when I was younger. Only, I had turned my energies to violence and revenge rather than sex and relationships.

"It's not only that. It's just, I..." I hesitated. I had no idea how to say it without just saying it. "I've never, you know. Done it. With a woman."

There. It was out there. It hung in the air like a particularly arid fart.

"You're gay?"

"What? No. What makes you think I am gay?"

"Wait, Halson, are you saying you've never had sex? You're a virgin?" She sounded genuinely shocked. "Wait, is this a celibacy thing? Are vampire hunters like priests? You aren't allowed to get laid?"

"Oh, God. No. Well, okay, there is some questionable lore about virgins being resistant to vampires, but nothing solid. Mostly, it's just that this lifestyle doesn't really leave a lot of time for much of a personal life. I mean, both my parents were vampire hunters, and so was my Uncle Dale, who took me in when they died. After what happened to my family, I learned it's not good to get too attached to people. You saw why today."

She stared at me. "What happened to your family?"

I started to answer, but my voice caught in my throat. Even after all these years, it was still raw. That wound, old and scarred over, was still tender. It was still fresh in my mind as I'd relived it a thousand times in my nightmares.

"It was just a few days before Christmas when I was nine. We were home from school on holiday. My mother and sister were baking cookies after dinner. I was playing on the living room floor with my older brother while my father was getting the fire started. It was our holiday tradition—we would all sit together on the couch and eat cookies while watching whatever Christmas special was on. Usually, it was some Rankin Bass picture. Then, there was a knock at the door. I think my dad thought it was Uncle Dale or a neighbor because he went to open the door even though it was late at night. He didn't take his gun or anything, so he wasn't ready when it happened."

I stopped as the memories brought back a flood of scents. Christmasy smells like gingerbread cookies, warm cocoa, and the sticky pine of the tree. It was all tainted with the acrid odor of smoke and the metallic tang of blood. I stifled a sniffle as my nose started to run, my eyes got hot, and I fought back tears.

"It was a vampire," I continued once I had control over myself again. "I don't know how it found us. My parents were careful, and the Order always took precautions, but it found us, anyway. I'm not sure if it was looking for revenge or just trying to wipe out vampire hunters in the area. I've never seen one like that. It was a true elder vampire, and it took pleasure in killing my family. It killed my brother outright, and took its time torturing my father by making him watch as it slowly killed my mother and sister."

"Oh, my God, how did you survive?" Her eyes filled with concern.

It was not an expression I'd ever seen from her before. She'd always been an unflappable badass. Alex had taken great care to present herself as the consummate, strong, independent woman. Today, however, had shown me the scared girl she must've been while growing up when the world was big and scary. She'd put on a stone façade in the face of a world that was hostile to women. It was a bit weird to see her softer, caring side, but it was nice. Almost nostalgic in a way, reminding me of how my mother and sister had been.

"I almost didn't," I replied, taking off my shirt and turning around so she could see the long, ragged scar on my back. It ran from between my shoulder blades, almost at the nape of my neck, down to the top of my tailbone. "It nearly ripped out my spine. I was in traction for almost a year. I don't know how I survived. I spent the better part of the next year relearning how to walk. My uncle Dale and his family took me in. I was so angry all the time for being too weak and helpless. That I couldn't do anything to save them. That it—the vampire—didn't even see me as a threat, like it was a waste of its time to actually kill me."

"Christ, Halson, you were nine. You were a little kid. Of course, there was nothing you could do. It was a monster, like that thing today. No one, especially a child, would have stood a chance. Darren is—*was*—a grown man who was built like a linebacker with combat training under his belt, and that thing...that thing killed him like it was nothing. You can't expect a child to—"

"I was fourteen when I killed my first vampire," I said matter-of-factly. "Not a Nosferatu, but still a pretty nasty and powerful one. I tracked and killed it by myself. It almost killed me."

She just stared at me as if she couldn't picture a short, skinny fourteen-year-old me, face full of acne and a voice that cracked, killing a full-blown monster. But I had. I'd reforged myself in the fires of anger and hate to avenge my parents. With single-minded focus, I'd honed myself to be the ideal killing machine that the Order envisioned for its hunters. A mortal man who could challenge all the creatures of the night and drive back the darkness.

"So, a virgin at your age..."

I shot her a dirty look, and she put up her hands in a don't-shoot-the-messenger way, giving me a goofy grin. She'd broken the tension my little backstory had built up. Now, both of us were sitting on her couch, shirtless.

Only one thing to do. Get the hell out of here.

Absolutely all sexual atmosphere was gone, which was probably for the best. Mistakes would've been made, and the good Lord knows I seem to love making them.

I put Alex to bed with some of the pain pills the EMTs had given her. She was gonna need real stitches beyond the temporary butterfly ones, and she'd have a scar, but the bandage they'd given her seemed to be working. I told her I would be on the couch if she needed anything, but she was out cold before I'd even shut the door.

So, I did the responsible thing and snuck out in shame.

And I didn't even get laid.

Chapter 12

I drove back to my office only to find it on fire. The whole building was ablaze. Instead of the three-story building, it was a three-story inferno.

I couldn't even think, I was so shell shocked. All I could do was stand there in the street and gawk with my mouth hanging open like I was trying to catch flies. After everything that had happened today, life still wasn't done kicking me while I was down. To be fair, that was pretty much life's go-to move.

I watched while firefighters ran back and forth, not trying to combat the blaze—it was pretty much a total loss—but to control it and keep it from spreading to the surrounding areas. And I just stood there like the world's biggest stopped clock. I could've been in bed having sex with a beautiful, albeit emotionally fragile, woman who wasn't against the idea. But no, I had to do the noble thing, and now I was being punished for it.

Way to go, Halson. Once again, the universe teaches you a really fucked up lesson that makes absolutely no sense.

I continued to stand in the middle of the street, watching my office building burn, until a cop came up to me and asked what I was doing there. I told him who I was and that it was my office building. When I asked him what happened, he shrugged and said some workman had called it in.

Looking around, I found the guy sitting in his truck. The police were wrapping up questioning him. I made my way over and pushed in after the cops left.

"Hey, buddy," I called. "You the guy who called in the fire?"

He looked up at me over an unlit cigarette. He was middle-aged, haggard with a deeply lined face, dressed in workman's overalls. His graying hair stuck out from under his painter's cap. His eyes had bags under them so large, they technically should've qualified as luggage. This was one of those salt-of-the-earth, hardworking types. Clearly not a firebug, not that I could tell.

"Yeah." His accent was rural Appalachian. "I got a late call from the building manager, an emergency job for window patch and estimate for a fitting."

Ah, so this was the glass guy Anita must've contacted. The actual building manager didn't do diddly squat, so we tenants took turns using his name to get various services out to do work, and then billing his holding company. As long as we used it sparingly, when needed, and played stupid when he came around asking about work orders he didn't sign, we pretty much got away with it.

"You got here, saw the fire, and called it in?" I asked.

"Yeah." He rolled the cigarette to the other side of his mouth without using his hands, a neat trick.

"You see anyone or anything?"

"Nope."

Oh, great. He was monosyllabic now. That was in no way, shape, or form gonna make asking questions tricky.

"So, you called in the fire and just sat here?"

He nodded in agreement with my statement.

"And?"

"Them cops said to stick around 'cause they had questions."

"What did they ask?"

"Same you did, I reckon. When did I get here, did I see anything, did I set the fire."

"Did you?"

He gave me a look like that was the dumbest question ever asked by a person.

"Okay, yeah, why set a fire and hang around for the cops to show up?"

"Yah knows firebugs love to hang around after they set a fire. They like to watch. Most of them tend to be firemen."

I looked around at the firefighters with suspicion after hearing his words. I quickly moved past that. None of the people here looked like they were here for shits and giggles. All the firefighters seemed beat to hell and back as they turned their attention to the main building once they had their parameters.

So, I hung out next to the guy's truck for the next hour as they put the blaze out and started poking through the rubble. The poor guy had to suffer along with me as the fire trucks had blocked him in. He was in the same boat. He did the right thing and got bit in the ass for it.

I put my hands into my coat pocket, and something sliced open the edge of my forefinger. I pulled out the piece of broken glass I'd taken from the office building and looked at it.

A bit of blood that looked black in the glow cast by the flashing lights ran along one sharp edge. I had been carrying it around all week and forgotten about it. I had a moment of inspiration and turned back to the workman.

"Hey, you know windows and glass right?"

"Yep, been installing them all my life." He was still sitting behind the wheel of his truck.

I leaned in the window and handed him the shard. "What can you tell me about this?"

He looked it over on both sides. Then turned it sideways and examined the cross-section. "Eh, we don't use this type of glass. We do mostly house windows, double-pane weather proofing, and stuff like that. Occasionally, we do plate glass for store fronts. This ain't none of that. This is safety glass, the kind they use in high-rise buildings."

"How can you tell?

He turned in his seat and showed me the edge of the shard. "See that line?" He pointed to the black line I'd noticed before. "That gives it away. What makes high-rise glass different is them tall buildings get constant direct sunlight from all angles. They use a specialized coated liner to cut down on UV to make it more tolerable. Think of it kinda like sunglasses for windows that people don't know is there."

Something in my brain clicked, but in the greater context of events, it made absolutely no sense.

This thought was almost instantly driven from my brain as several firefighters came out of the burned, smoldering building with a body bag on a stretcher. The bottom fell out of my stomach as I watched the fire marshal signal the ambulance crew to take the body away.

It felt like slow motion as I approached the fire marshal, asked what had happened, and whose body they had taken away.

He was a short, heavy-set man with a walrus-like mustache. He checked his clipboard before confirming what I'd feared. The body they found was on the third floor, in my office, and of a large African-American woman. It appears as if several bottle bombs of some kind had been thrown through the windows of the plumbing store on the bottom floor. The flames had cut off the stairs and flooded the upper floors with smoke. They believed she died of smoke inhalation while trying to exit the building.

Anita must have stayed late to make sure the window repairman showed up. She had just been doing her job, and it had cost her life. What was it about me that I just kept getting people killed?

I sat on the curb in stunned silence. I tried to cry. I wanted to cry, but all I could feel was that stupid, hot ball of hatred building up again in the pit of my stomach. I wanted to throw up. I wanted to punch something. I wanted to make someone pay for this. I wanted to make that person hurt for every little thing that had gone wrong in the last few weeks. I wanted to vent my fury on the world.

It was still dark in the early morning when the last fire truck finally rolled away. I didn't even look up. I just sat there with my head between my knees. Finally, alone, I let out a primal scream of anger that vanished into the night along with the flashing lights. It didn't make me feel any better. I just wanted to go to bed to black out, not think for several hours, then eat something, and finally, maybe, find the asshole responsible and set them on fire. See how they liked it.

When I finally got up, my knees popped, and my back was stiff and sore from sitting on the cold concrete, but I forced myself. As I made my way across the street toward my car, bright lights snapped on and blinded me. Like an idiot, I looked, bringing up one hand to shield my eyes.

There came the unmistakable roar of an engine revving, and I knew what that meant.

Still half-blind, I hobbled towards the Road Runner and dove over the hood at the last second. An old pickup truck side-swiped the car just as I cleared it.

Pulling to a halt, someone stuck a Mac10 out the driver's side window, and there came a sound like a manic woodpecker on meth trying to tunnel through a metal pole. Several very fast-moving objects whipped past me by inches, sounding like angry hornets.

After firing the machine pistol empty, the truck took off. By the time I stuck my head up over the hood of the car, they were long gone.

I hadn't gotten a look at the license plate or the driver. I had no clue who was taking potshots at me, but I had a strong suspicion it was the same someone who shot out the office windows and burned the place down.

I could have given chase, and the little hate-monster in my stomach wanted to, but I had bigger fish to fry.

And when I looked at the poor Road Runner, she had about half a dozen new holes in her. Days like this, I was actually happy I didn't have car insurance.

Chapter 13

When I got back to Alex's apartment, I took a few of her painkillers and passed out on the couch. I didn't wake up until around five the next evening. I'd been exhausted, as had Alex, and when we woke up, we realized it had been almost twenty-four hours since either of us had eaten anything, so we hit up a locally-owned Waffle House knock-off.

I had the big breakfast plate—biscuits and gravy with sausage, half a pound of bacon, four fried eggs, loaded hash browns, and a large glass of orange juice. Alex had what I can only describe as diabetes on a plate. It was some fancy, deep-fried French toast and powdered sugar waffles, topped with whipped cream, and smothered in maple syrup with a chocolate milkshake. Just looking at it made my teeth ache.

"Holy crap, how can you eat that much sugar? If I ate that much in one sitting, I'd be so hyped up, I could see the flow of time." How did this woman eat like a five-year-old without supervision and still maintain her fitness magazine body?

"Says you," she retorted. "You're going to need to spend four hours on the toilet after all that meat. That is, if you don't have a heart attack first."

"I will have you know this is a very scientifically designed diet, especially for vampire hunters. It keeps us alert and with plenty of protein to build monster-fighting muscle. It's not for mere mortals."

Alex rolled her eyes and dug into her food.

I did the same, and it was Heaven. Greasy, salty, and delicious. I had killed most of the plate before looking up to lock gazes with Alex, who'd been in the midst of a similar orgasmic food dilemma. Once our eyes met, it turned into a childish race to see who could finish first.

By the time we were done eating, we were both sweating and full to bursting. Alex ordered us more coffee as I undid my belt a few notches so my stomach would stop hurting. We burped, we farted, and did all the post-meal, ate-too-much nastiness.

"So, about the vampire hunting stuff..."

I rolled my eyes. Here came the questions.

"So, like, how do you, like, get into it? Do you have to be born in a bloodline? Or are you specially chosen? I know you said your whole family were vampire hunters."

"No, it's not like that. Anyone can train and become a vampire hunter. Most are orphaned survivors taken in by the Order. Yeah, there are vampire hunter families and bloodlines, but my family was more the exception to the rule. Only my parents and my uncle were part of the Order that I know of. My brother and sister were too young, but my brother had started training."

"What's the Order like?" Alex leaned in, listening intently as she sipped a fresh cup of coffee.

"From what I've seen, it's mostly just a bunch of old, fat guys who sit around telling war stories while the younger crowd get sent off to die pointlessly. They aren't really that organized for a group who calls themselves 'The Order'." I sipped my coffee. It tasted burned like the pot was left on too long.

"All order and no order."

"Basically. We're just people, after all."

"So, do you get special abilities and stuff?"

"Oh yeah, we can totally fly and walk through walls. It all comes with a secret decoder ring." I snarked.

"Jesus, okay, you don't have to be a dick about it." Her forehead furrowed at my curtness, and I instantly felt like a dick.

I sighed. "Have you ever seen me do anything special or out of the ordinary?" I took another sip.

"Well, no, but honestly, we never really spend much time together. I've never really seen you hunt. No one outside Bullard really has. Most of the guys in the unit think you're nuts." She brushed a random strand of her hair behind her ear.

I hadn't thought about it, but I had really shut her and the other cops out. "Did you ever hear how me and Bullard started working together?"

"No, and Bullard never talked about it. He just said you were the real deal, and to stand back and just let you do your thing." She leaned forward again in interest.

"It was a couple of years ago. Before Bullard had taken over the unit, and I was still operating mostly under the radar. There was this wannabe vampire groupie. Fat, greasy, little rat when he was human, you know the type. Total loser, angsty, blamed others for his faults, etcetera, etcetera. After he became a vampire, I felt sorry for the vamp who did that deed. He tried to reinvent himself as some sort of Lestat knockoff—dressed in old-timey clothing, spoke in a British accent, and just being weird."

She laughed.

I shook my head. "You laugh, but he started building himself a little cult, and people were buying it. Of course, it helped he was a vampire, so his lackeys totally fell for it. They start running around, committing crimes for their 'master'. Petty stuff, shoplifting, vandalism, and the like. They were young adults and easily impressionable. But then they hit the big time. At some point, this guy figured out he could use his vampire powers to rob the armored cars that run at night.

"Things kick off, they rob a couple of trucks, and no one can figure out how they're doing it. One time, they go too far, and the vampire kills one of the armored guards, who happened to be a retired cop—a retired cop with ties to our favorite loser unit. The guy was Bullard's old training officer. He took it personally, and after his higher-ups told him to drop it, he decided to go a little off the reservation, and work this case on his own.

"Bullard was determined because he found the vampire's lair. To be fair, it was due to their own stupidity. Instead of just robbing the truck, they stole one."

"Wait, they didn't think the truck had GPS on it?" Alex interjected, and I pointed my finger at her in agreement.

"Bingo. The idiots didn't realize the trucks are tracked. Bullard tracked the truck back to their hideout. At that same time, your favorite vampire hunter was tracking down the vampire through ancient and mysterious methods."

"Oh, bullshit. I bet you just got lucky." She snickered.

"Meh, basically. I just looked at all the hijack sites on a map, drew a circle around the area that covered all of them, and searched all the abandoned and empty buildings in that area. But yeah, I got lucky and just happened to be moving in on the hideout at the same time as Bullard.

"However, Bullard thought they were just regular criminals and had no clue what he was getting himself into. He, and the guys he convinced to go with him, moved in, thinking they were raiding a regular crime ring. Things went his way at first. They went in and rounded up the kids. Then things hit the fan when the sun went down, and the vampire woke up. He tore through the other six men like they were tissue paper.

"Final standoff was Bullard and this vamp. On the one hand, you have Bullard, who is an absolute mountain of a man, decked out in full tactical gear. On the other, you've got this little poser vampire, couldn't have been more than five-foot three, lank, oily hair, way too much goth makeup. Think if *The Crow* had been played by Seth Green. It couldn't have been more hilarious, except the vampire had gone all murder machine on six other cops. Bullard never stood a chance. That is, until yours truly arrived and totally saved the day."

"Oh, I can't wait to hear this." Her voice dripped with sarcasm.

"Hey, who's telling the story? Okay, you weren't there, so you don't know how incredibly amazing and brave and heroic I looked."

She cocked an eyebrow at me.

"Alright, I hit him in the face with a water balloon full of holy water while hiding behind an old industrial washing machine. The place had been a laundry mat at one time. Anyways, Bullard and I managed to back him into the stolen armored truck. I pitched a Molotov cocktail inside, then we shut the back doors, and Bullard used his shotgun to wedge them shut while we roasted the vampire alive. He burned to ash, and the day was saved."

"What happened next?"

"Well, Bullard, disobeying his higher-up, getting cops killed, and someone, not pointing any fingers, accidentally burned up the money in the back of the truck with the vampire... Yeah, he got a one-way ticket to the loser's club in the PSIC unit. Unlike everyone else, he did his job a little too well, got promoted to lead the unit, and got me hired on as a consultant to clean up things."

When I finished, we both just kinda sat back and let it sink in. I don't think I'd ever told that story to anyone before, and it was clear Bullard hadn't told anyone, either. I was staring into the depths of my coffee mug and wished he was here with us. Then, I remembered Anita, and my heart had pangs of guilt. Two people on the same day. I had gotten two people I cared about killed.

"So, let's hear it," I said, breaking the silence.

"Hear what?" Alex blinked at me in confusion. Her eyes, even in this light, were stunning.

"Let's hear your story and how you ended up working with Bullard in the dumb-dumb tank." I smirked, half expecting her to refuse.

"Okay, you know how I used to be white-collar, right?"

"I recall it being mentioned, and then I was threatened. Violently, might I add."

She just rolled her eyes again and ignored me. "I joined the Philly PD after college, where I got degrees in criminal justice and finance."

I whistled. Pretty and smart.

"Yeah, shut up. I got sent to white-collar crimes. I didn't want to waste time busting street dealers. The true criminals are on Wall Street. You want to crack down on the power players, the people who run real organized crime, top men, you hit them in the pocketbook."

"That's how they got Capone, right?"

"Technically, yep. For tax evasion. You don't mess with Treasury. Money makes people do stupid things. Lots of money makes people do *really* stupid things. And busting those people can make some cops do really stupid things, like trying to get a business partner of a religious extremist cult to flip by harassing his loser son."

I whistled again. "I know where this is going."

"Yeah." She brushed hair behind her ear again. "Daddy put a bug in the mayor's ear. The mayor shits on the police commissioner. The police commissioner shits on the police chief, and…"

"Ugh, I get it. It's turtles all the way down."

"Bingo, Halson. I got bumped to the 'loser squad' as you put it. Bullard recognizes my hard work and potential as a good cop, and takes me under his wing. Until one day, this asshole comes along and slaps my ass."

"In my defense, it was a very firm ass." I offered her one of my trademark Halson shit-eating grins.

"Thank you." She kicked me in the shin under the table.

"So, why become a cop?" I asked. "You're smart, pretty, well-educated, and know how to get what you want. Why be a cop? You could be anyone or anything, but you chose a low-paying, civil-servant job. I ain't buying it."

"My dad was a cop." That was it, plain and simple. Too simple.

"There's more to it than that. Come on, just say you can't beat my backstory. I got the whole tragic family thing, and you can't top it."

She leaned across the table and stared deep into my eyes. "When I was twelve and my older sister was sixteen, she was kidnapped by a cult, and we never saw her again. After two years in hell of stalled investigations and higher-ups road-blocking the case, my father put his service weapon in his mouth and blew his brains out at our kitchen table while everyone was away. I was the one who found his body when I came home from school. Is that tragic enough for you, Halson? You don't have the market cornered on sad backstories." She glared at me.

Shit. "Oh, wow. I'm an asshole."

"Yes, you are, Halson, but they say the first step is admitting it."

She leaned back and rolled her coffee cup between her hands, and I honestly couldn't tell if she was playing me or not. That was a horrifyingly haunting story, delivered with the weight of someone who'd lived it. I was almost sure she hadn't made it up to mess with me, but I just sat there in stunned silence for a second.

"So, these B&B guys, they're bad, right? In the financial world?"

"Yes and no," she responded. "No, in that what they do is the norm, so that makes them no worse than any other corporate pirates. They're all cut from the same cloth. But yes, what they do is evil, and they wreck people's lives just for the sake of a little more profits on the company spreadsheets."

Hearing that made something go off in my head, and I dug through my pockets. I pulled everything out. Knives, lint, change, pack of Lifesavers. Finally, I found it. A couple of crumpled-up pieces of paper. I unfolded them before trying to flatten them and make them decent.

"What's that?" She looked at the pages I'd excavated.

"Not sure. You're the financial wizard, you tell me." I handed her the papers, and she spent the next few minutes glaring at them instead of me.

"Where did you get these?"

"Donald Baker's office. They were in his printer. What are they?"

"You stole evidence from an active crime scene?"

"First off, not active. Second, not stole, borrowed. Now what is it?"

She grumped in her seat, still looking over the crumpled pages before answering. "They're some sort of financial transaction records. Money going in and out of the company. Deals are being made, and bills are being paid. So on and so forth. But he's marked two different kinds of transfers." She elaborated, pointing to the red and green lines.

"Okay, what kind of transfers?" I asked, still completely lost.

"I don't know. Without the company's record guide, I can't say for sure, but if the red is money going out, and green is money coming in, there's more going out than coming in."

"And that's bad? Like, kill a man bad?"

She nodded and looked up at me. "Halson, reports like this, in my experience, usually are evidence of embezzlement."

"Oh yeah, I think you said something about how there are consequences to stealing from the rich."

She let out a sigh. "Yeah, and without access to the company records, we can't prove anything or catch the person doing it."

"Hold that thought. What time and day is it?" I asked, checking Alex's watch.

"Thursday, almost seven. Why?" Her tone was suspicious as though I was about to pull a rabbit out of a very inappropriate place.

"I may have a man on the inside."

Chapter 14

Alex and I arrived at the B&B building at a time when most sane people were heading home to escape their soul-crushing jobs. Sane people, or at least, those who weren't dead inside and had nothing else to live for. I took Alex up to the accounting floor, hoping my man would still be there. From what I could remember, he should still be at his desk.

The accounting floor was a maze of identical cubicles stretching out in every conceivable direction imaginable. It was a sea of identical conformity designed to strip people of their will to live. I felt like I'd stepped into a Dilbert comic as we moved through the cubicles, looking for Lenny's desk. Most of them were empty. Anyone with a life had probably bolted out the door the second the clock hands hit drinking time.

They were all the same. A chair, a computer, and a phone, but what differed were the personal items. Some people had tried to counter the soul-sucking horror of banality with tasteful knickknacks and pictures of their families. I wasn't sure if I liked humanizing these people until I realized that was probably the same thought their bosses had for them.

I couldn't imagine working in a place like this. I mean *holy hell,* the same thing day in and day out for the rest of your life. It would be torture. Plus, I don't look good in khaki. Okay, I don't look good in anything, least of all khaki.

My man was in. There was a glow from his computer screen in the darkened room. I had no clue why he was sitting in the dark, other than, this late at night, the building probably shuts off the lights to save on the power bill or something.

We wound our way through the network of miniature walls. Lenny didn't seem to hear us coming. Either he was really engrossed in his work or really good at sleeping while sitting up at his desk.

"You know, it's seen as rude to watch internet porn at work." I leaned against his cubicle wall.

He nearly jumped out of his skin. "I'm not...I wasn't..." His face was flushed with sweat breaking out on his forehead.

I'd found out Lenny stayed late on Thursdays to catch up on work from the days he left early to visit his mother in the hospital. So, I knew we could catch him here after hours and lean on him for information while no one was around.

"Watcha doin', little buddy?" I craned to look at his monitor. It wasn't porn. It was worse. Spreadsheets. Mindless, identical columns of meaningless numbers marched across his screen. I don't know how he spends hours a day looking at this. After just five seconds, it made my brain want to explode.

"J-just doing work."

He seemed nervous, but I chalked that up to being accosted by the two of us alone at night.

"Neat. What can you tell us about this?"

Lenny pushed his glasses up his nose and squinted at the crumpled pages I handed him. He tried smoothing them out some, but the wrinkles were pretty much set in at this point. His lips moved as he scanned one page and then the other.

"So?" I asked.

"So?" he repeated. "They're financial transaction sheets. So what?" He shrugged and turned back to his computer.

"Aren't you an accountant? Can't you tell us anything about them?"

"I'm an accountant, yes, but not a wizard. I can't tell you more without more information. I need to know what they're referencing, what business, and what kinds of transactions before I can start diagnosing anything. I really can't help you." He shrugged again, minimized his spreadsheet, then pulled up the computer game he must've been playing and had hidden when we arrived.

"Come on, man. Nothing? What if I told you it was from the B&B accounts. Would that give you any idea?"

He paused the game and looked at me, clearly interested. "B&B? Well, we do their in-house accounting, so we have access to their books, but..."

"But what?" I did not like him jerking me around like this, especially with Alex watching me do a whole amateur-hour routine.

"I would need police authorization and a warrant to show any kind of personal financial data about a client."

"Well, good news. Officer Benson here is from the Philly PD. She worked white-collar crimes and is on the Baker case. So, let's get a look at those files." I reached for the mouse and left out which unit Alex worked for now, and the scope of her jurisdiction, leading him to believe whatever.

He swatted my hand away. "Nope, I need to see a badge and a warrant."

Alex didn't so much as badge him as she almost rammed it up his nose. "Here is my badge, and if you want a warrant, I can go get one, come back, and shove it so far up your ass, it will be the most sexual contact you've had since the first time you touched yourself. Or you can voluntarily show me the files while remembering your head is the right height to get bounced off this desk."

She went full "bad cop" on him. I also noticed she didn't correct him as to the true nature of her police affiliation, either.

"I can't do that." He whimpered, and she glared at him. "But, I mean, if I was looking at the files and you just happened to glance over my shoulder, then there's nothing I could do..."

"That's a good boy," she replied.

I swear, he gave her a look like he was about to get on the floor and start licking her boots. It made me feel unclean and in need of a shower.

He turned back to his computer and started clicking through files. Eventually, his screen was filled with a different set of columns and numbers, which I couldn't make head or tails of, but Alex and Lenny were really interested in.

"So, you see here?" He highlighted a line of numbers. "That's money going into the account."

"From where?" Alex asked.

"Dunno. Clients, sales, foreign banks, doesn't matter."

"Why not?"

"Because you see here?" He highlighted another group of numbers. "The money goes out in minutes."

I frowned. "Okay, so money goes in, and money goes out. So what? Isn't that just finance?"

Lenny and Alex looked at me like I was the class dunce who'd stopped eating paste in order to ask a stupid question.

"No, not even close." Lenny scooted, clearly enjoying he had something over me to impress Alex with. He highlighted a third line. "Here, the money comes right back into the account, the same amount that just went out."

Alex narrowed her eyes at the screen in concentration.

"Uh, okay? What does that mean?" I was clearly the dumb one who needed things explained.

"It usually means money laundering," Alex explained. "The money comes in, it goes out to some shell companies, gets bounced all over the globe, and then, more or less, it's clean."

"Incorrect." Lenny smiled smugly, happy he apparently thought he was the smartest person in the room.

Alex shot him a questioning glance.

"It's the same account, but the amount doesn't change."

I could swear the little creep was staring at Alex's breasts when she wasn't looking, and I was about to smack him, but to be fair, she was currently practicing the philosophy of "if they are flawless, you can go braless," and I was having a hard time not sneaking looks myself. Hey, I was a thirteen-year-old boy once.

I like boobs. Sue me.

"That's not unusual," she remarked.

"No, you don't get it. In money laundering, the amount changes. Usually, it shrinks due to costs and currency exchanges, right?"

She nodded in agreement, obviously following his line of logic.

"But this amount doesn't change. It doesn't even grow. Money accumulates, but in this account, it never goes above a certain amount. When it does, it's cleaned out, and that same base amount is put back in. Money comes in, the account empties, and then the exact same amount appears back in the account out of thin air."

"Wait, so the returned amount is always the same, despite how much goes into the account?" Alex scanned the paper sheets and compared them to the screen, matching colored line for line.

Lenny hit a key, lighting up all the similar transactions. It wasn't a lot, but it was enough that even I could see it was fishy.

"So, where's the money going? The extra money, I mean," I asked.

Lenny shrugged. "Dunno. I don't have access to routing numbers and bank codes. This is basically just a digital balance sheet. Whoever was doing this is an idiot."

"What do you mean?" I asked, slightly offended.

"This is baseline, old school, book cooking." He leaned back in his chair. "You would put the number in the book, then go back, erase it, and put in a new number, minus the amount you skimmed. With old paper books, this was pretty common and easy. Whoever is doing this doesn't seem to know how computers work, that they keep a log of these changes. This person is basically computer illiterate because they just delete the old number and type in a new one without realizing the computer records the change."

"So, we're looking for someone's grandma?" I asked.

Both Alex and Lenny looked at me.

"What? I know how to use a computer. I made my own website. Why do people always look shocked when they find out I can actually use technology?"

"Probably because you look like a neolithic throwback."

I was about to smack Lenny for that comment, and to protect Alex's honor from his lecherous stares, but mostly over the comment, when his head picked that exact moment to explode.

His computer monitor and the walls of his cubicle were covered with blood, brains, and bits of skull fragments.

Alex and I froze in shock, caught completely flat-footed. I blinked and stared at what was left of him. You don't expect something like that to happen, even with a life as wild as mine.

"Get your fucking hands up!"

The voice didn't register at first. I couldn't tear my eyes away from Lenny's body as it slumped in the chair before crashing to the floor.

Looking up, a short, stocky man in a shaggy, shapeless coat had a baseball cap pulled down low on his head. He stood a couple cubicles away. I couldn't figure out where I knew this guy from. His hands had my attention and jogged my memory. He held a MAC-10 machine pistol in his good hand with his support hand in a cast.

The last time I'd seen him, EMTs were taking him to the hospital because I'd broken his arm.

"Um, Alex, who is this guy again?" The question was asked over my shoulder as we both turned to face him and raised our hands. I wasn't giving this prick any satisfaction. I wanted him to know how insignificant he was to me.

"He's that little bitch guard you beat up twice and got fired, Halson." Alex growled, following my lead. "You really don't remember?"

"Do you remember every piece of shit you scraped off your shoe?"

If we got him frustrated, he might slip up and give us a chance to run, or turn the tables on him. Alex and I were packing, but he had the edge in firepower and the jump on us. We weren't in a good position. If we made the wrong misstep, he could easily blast us with that little machine gun of his, and that would be it for us.

Luckily, guys like him were more ego than brains, so it was a decent gamble considering that, in the last twenty-four hours, he'd burned down my office, killed my secretary, and taken shots at me. It was safe to say he wasn't planning on leaving us alive. Especially since he'd just killed Lenny in front of a cop. Nope, he was going to tie up loose ends, eliminate the witnesses, and get a little payback. It's what I would've done if I'd been an angry little ego-maniacal sociopath.

"Yeah, Halson. Piss off the guy holding a gun on us." Alex snarled.

"Hey, you called him a little bitch and made fun of his small penis."

"Are you trying to get us killed?" she shouted in mock disbelief.

She was really selling it. She had some talent as an actress. My acting skills sucked. I usually fall back on being a jerk.

"And I didn't say anything about his obvious micro-penis."

The guard's face screwed up in anger. I'm not sure what was getting to him more, our comments or that we were almost ignoring him.

The portion of his face below the cap turned beet red. He bared his teeth, spit flying from his mouth, his eyes rolling madly in his head. "*Shut up*! Shut up! Shut up! Shut up!"

"Someone's got their panties in a bunch," Alex said sardonically, rolling her eyes as if he were just any old man-baby throwing a tantrum.

He grew more flustered, thrashing his torso back and forth. He did look like a child throwing a temper tantrum.

We seized the opportunity at almost the same time. Alex went for her police-issue Glock at the small of her back as I went into my jacket for the .45 in its shoulder holster.

We had barely managed to clear our respective holsters when the little machine pistol let out another of those devastating burps, spraying the carpet at our feet with bullets and up along one of the cubicle walls to our right. Poor Lenny's body caught a few stray rounds as the belligerent former security guard made his point.

We both froze instantly.

"*Drop 'em!*" He brandished the MAC 10 at us, smoke still curling from the barrel.

I couldn't tell how many rounds he had left. The shots had been too fast to count, and I wasn't sure how many rounds the magazines held. I also didn't know if that was a warning shot or if his aim was just that bad, but we weren't taking any chances.

"*Drop 'em,*" he screamed again, and we did.

I tried to drop my 1911 in a way that would hopefully discharge and hit the guy, but no such luck. The old gun was built too well and the safety features kept it from going off. I had more hope for Alex's dinky plastic 9mm, but it just thumped uselessly to the floor.

We stood there, now disarmed at the psychopath's mercy, and with no more options. My backup plan was to tackle the guy when he got close enough, and hope that Alex could beat the shit out of him while he was busy filling me full of holes. I don't know what her plan was, but it had to be better than mine.

The guard looked at her and gestured towards me with the gun. "Hit him."

"Excuse me?"

"Oh yeah, excuse you?" I added.

"I said, *hit him*. Knock him out." The little guy growled.

"What? Are you nuts? This isn't a cartoon. It doesn't work like that. You could easily kill someone."

I was a little touched by the concern, but saw a golden opportunity.

He stepped forward and aimed the gun at her. He was smart enough to stay just out of reach, but he was close enough that, even with the unreliable accuracy of the MAC-10, he wouldn't fail to kill her.

"No, Benson, go ahead and do it," I said calmly.

"What? Did you suddenly catch the stupid, too?" She glared as if she found herself to be the only sane adult in the room.

"Just do it, or else he's going to shoot us."

"Of course, you were born with a terminal case of the stupid, Halson."

As she hefted a heavy binder from a nearby desk, I hoped she got my message when I'd used her last name in a serious tone. Alex would hit me, I would go down, playing dead, or unconscious in this case, and then the idiot would lower his guard as he focused only on her. Then, I could pop up from playing possum, maybe grab one of our guns, and pull a totally sick *Die Hard* move, complete with a badass one-liner.

"Come on, what's one more brain injury? I've had like a doz—"

I don't know if she didn't realize my plan, hit me too hard, or maybe after so many head injuries, my skull had gone soft, but when she slammed the binder into the base of my skull, my lights went out for real.

Chapter 15

I was back in nightmare land again. Nine years old, sprawled out on the living room floor of my childhood home, crippled and watching my family die all over again. Those nightmares were always so vivid. The screams, the blood, the pain, the terror. Over and over. My own personal hell played out on the screen of my mind to torture myself every time I closed my eyes.

This time, it was particularly nasty. I could smell the smoke and feel the heat as the house burned around me. Flames licked the walls and ceiling as smoke hung thick and dark in the room. No one was coming to save me. If the blood loss or vampire didn't kill me first, the fire and smoke would. And through that smoke were the vampire's burning, glowing eyes, retreating into dense smoke.

That was a new twist to the dream. Usually, it would loom up out of the dark, fangs bared to devour me. But this time, it was backing away into the night as the flames grew hotter and hotter. Too hot. I could feel them on my face.

"Halson! Wake your dumb ass up!"

Why was Alex in my dream? No, seriously, what the heck was going on?

I slowly dragged myself from the depths of unconsciousness. My head was fuzzy, and there was a sharp pain in the top of my neck. When I shook my head, my skull went loose, and everything went all watery. I instantly stopped and waited for the spinning to stop.

"What the hell happened?" I asked, still groggy and trying to get my brain to understand what I was looking at.

"Jesus, you're a lightweight, Halson." Her voice came from my left and just out of sight behind me.

I tried to turn and look at her, but I couldn't move. I'd been bound with a combination of duct tape and electrical cords. My hands were restrained behind me with ziptie handcuffs, and my back was pressed against something not unpleasantly soft and moving.

"How is it my fault you hit me with all of your gorilla strength?"

"I barely tapped you. You get knocked out easier than a leading lady in a noir film. You're one step up from sniffing handkerchiefs to see if they smell like chloroform."

Looking around, I realized where we were. We were sitting on the floor in a janitor's closet. It was like all the others in the building I'd been in. Bare, stark, a plastic utility sink, and a row of shelving units with cleaning supplies.

And, of course, those shelves were on fire. Because life never misses a chance to kick me in the balls when I'm down.

It wasn't very big yet, but it was growing. The concrete wall didn't burn, but the flames were climbing up the metal shelving unit as more items caught fire. Once it reached the false ceiling, things were going to get real bad, real quick. The blue-gray smoke was already billowing toward the top of the room. Thankfully, we were sitting on the floor, so we weren't choking on it yet. If we didn't get out soon, we would suffocate.

"How long was I out?" I tested the tape binding me. It was strong stuff, and there was a lot of it, but it was just tape. All I needed was time. Unfortunately, I was running out of that quickly.

"I dunno, fifteen minutes, I guess." She spoke over my shoulder. "After he made me knock you out, he had me drag you into the closet, then he tied us up and set the room on fire before he left. You woke up a few minutes later."

"Oh well, that's good. I wasn't out that long."

"Halson, there is *no* good length of time to be unconscious. You really should see a doctor if we get out of this alive. I don't know how your head can be full of anything but mashed potatoes at this point."

I snorted. She wasn't wrong. I started shifting my weight back and forth as I moved my legs, trying to kick off my right boot.

"What are you doing?" She hissed at me.

I leaned back into her a little too hard. "Trying to get free."

"Does that involve rolling on top of me?"

"I'm trying to get my boot off. I have a straight razor in there I can use to cut us free."

"Oh. That's pretty clever."

"Thanks," I muttered, rolling my eyes as my boot finally came off and I flipped it over.

Nothing fell out.

"What?" she demanded.

"Nothing. Must've put it in the left boot."

She sighed. "Only thing I have in my boot is a little .38."

"Wait, you have a *gun*?" I moaned, exasperated, as I managed to get the razor out of my boot. "Why didn't you used it before that whack job locked us in the closet?"

"I didn't get a chance. He had his gun on you the whole time. I couldn't risk it."

For a second, it actually sounded like she almost gave a shit about what happened to me.

"Wow, I'm touched you care that much."

"I swear to God, Halson, if we die in here, I'm going to shoot you myself."

I snickered as I scooted the razor under me and into my hands. It easily cut through the zipties and tape. It just came apart with the lightest touch from the razor. The cords I slipped over my head.

Seriously, never use electrical cords to tie people up. They are terrible for that.

I cut Alex free just as easily.

The door to the closet was either locked or blocked, but only for about a second. We put our boots to the door in unison, and the whole thing came off its hinges and fell into the hallway.

Fleeing the burning utility closet, we made our way back into the office full of cubicles when Alex suddenly grabbed me, yanking me off my feet. We crashed to the ground behind one of the cubicles as the aisle we were in was replaced with a wall of bullets.

Oh, great. Our arsonist was still here. The cubicle walls did nothing to stop the 9mm hailstorm of machine gun fire. They did, however, hide us from his lines of sight, and like most amateurs, he was firing blind and aiming at about waist height. So, as long as we stayed low to the ground, all his shots were above our heads.

"He has us pinned down. What do we do?" I peeked around the corner and nearly lost an eye when he sprayed the cubicle with gunfire.

He was in the middle of the room, standing on a desk, allowing him to look over the cubicles. It was an excellent tactical position. It gave him the high ground, and while he couldn't fully see over the walls, he could see enough to rain bullets in almost any direction. He had a nearly three hundred and sixty degree field of fire, and would see anything coming.

Alex pulled the small revolver from her ankle holster and rolled the cylinder open to check it. Snapping it closed, she glanced back at me.

I held out my hand for the gun, and she gave me a confused get-out-of-here glare.

"What do you think you're doing?"

"You give me the gun, I'll distract him, and you run for help."

She looked at me like I'd lost my mind.

"Don't get all chauvinistic on me, Halson. I can take care of myself," she hissed defensively.

"Not what I meant," I hissed back.

"How about you distract him, and I shoot him?"

"You want me to be bait?" I snapped as we crawled along the floor, trying to keep moving so he couldn't draw a proper bead on us.

"You make great bait, Halson. Everyone wants to shoot you."

She pulled up short and peeked around a corner. In front of us was an open aisle, and crossing it would leave us open to gunfire as we gave away our position.

She gave me a pointed look, and with some hesitation, I took off running. I crossed the open aisle and was behind the opposite cubicle when gunfire started.

He turned as he fired, and bullets ripped through the faux walls just inches behind me.

I kept running until I came to the next intersection. I juked to my right, before going down the aisle to my left. It bought me a few seconds as he had to course-correct his aim. The further I went, the further his attention was from Alex.

I was seconds from getting shot when he finally gave her enough of his back that she could pop up and take a shot without him instantly turning the machine gun on her.

The .38 fired and the MAC-10 stopped chattering.

I turned, hoping to see him down, but instead, he was examining a hole in the sleeve of his jacket.

She'd missed, but not by much. Before she could get off another shot, he turned the pistol on her, forcing her to retreat to the safety of the cubical maze.

Grabbing a stapler, I hucked it at his head, grazing his ear. It got his attention, and he turned the Mac on me again. I dove below his line of sight and crawled down the rest of the row as bullets tore through the walls above me.

There came a commotion, the gunfire stopped coming at me, and it went in another direction.

Apparently, Alex had tried to get him again, but this time, he'd been ready, and she hadn't had time to get a shot off.

We spent the next several minutes playing a psychotic version of whack-a-mole for keeps. I kept trying to get his attention so he would give Alex an opening, but after a couple of attempts, he caught on and started ignoring me for the most part. He must've figured out I was just a distraction, and Alex was the only one of us armed with a real weapon.

We couldn't keep this up all night. Getting desperate, I yanked a desk printer off its connection cables and chucked it at him with all my strength. Up until this point, I'd been throwing small items. Coffee cups, picture frames, binders. Anything I could lob at him for attention.

He hadn't been expecting a twenty-pound printer. It crashed into him at about hip level, knocking him off the desk. He crashed to the floor with a burst of gunfire into the ceiling. He must've accidentally pulled the trigger when he'd landed.

Alex's head popped up on the other side of the room as she took a chance to look at what happened.

I pointed and signaled that he was down.

She nodded and then vanished again.

In the middle of the room, the gunman struggled to his feet and pulled a fresh clip from his pocket, loading it into the MAC-10 and snapping the bolt.

How much ammo did this guy have? It felt like he was firing at us nonstop. Granted, I'd been too busy running around trying not to die to count his reloads.

Ducking before he could spot me, I started duck-walking to the end of my row. Reaching it, I risked a quick look. Standing up, I was a head taller than the cubicles. They hit me around my shoulders. The guard was so short, all I could spot was the top of his head and ears as he moved around. He'd given up staying in one place and playing defense. He was on the hunt. It was a lot more dangerous for everyone.

If Alex or I stood up, it could give away our positions, but if we moved around in a crouch, we couldn't see each other or him. We also couldn't call out to one another without giving away our locations. Meanwhile, he could stalk around almost completely at random, and if he ran into one of us, we would be ventilated.

He couldn't hit anything with that little SMG from a distance, but that's not what it was designed for. The MAC-10 had been designed for CIA agents in tight spots operating in urban and indoor environments. It excelled at killing in close combat encounters exactly like this. Our only real hope was if Alex could get the drop on him and shoot him before he could react. Anything else, and he would be the only one walking out of here.

I continued scurrying around the room, completely losing all sense of direction. Everything looked the same. I took a chance at another peek over the wall, and things were going from bad to worse.

Somehow, as the three of us played hide and seek, we got turned around. The next row over, Alex was crouched and moving toward an intersection. Around the corner, coming from the opposite direction, was the guard. Judging by their relative speeds, they would meet at roughly the same time in the intersection. With no cover, it would be down to a contest of reaction times.

While I had every confidence in her speed, beating him out in a fair match-up, we live in the real world where survival isn't about fairness and who's better. It's he who cheats that wins.

I was gonna give her every advantage I could. Getting a running start, I vaulted onto a desk and launched myself over the wall at the guard. He didn't see me coming until the last second with no time to react. I landed on him in a sort of quasi-body slam that was ninety percent bellyflop like an old-school pro wrestler. It wasn't pretty, but it did the job.

We collapsed in a pile of my gangly limbs and his baggy clothes. He came down on his firing arm, pinning the machine gun beneath him. With me on top, he couldn't do anything to free it, so he was forced to resort to hitting me with his injured arm. From that angle, he couldn't get much leverage to generate power. But he was hitting me with his cast, and getting hit with a cast is like getting smacked with a brick. They're hard, and it hurts. He fetched several good licks to the face before my berserker rage reached a level where I could power through and start rabbit-punching him in the side of the head and neck.

We tussled on the ground like a couple of kids in a schoolyard squabble. The whole time, he made this high-pitched keening noise like a stuck pig. Neither one of us was able to get an advantage.

I didn't know what Alex was up to, but there was no way she could've gotten a shot off at the guard with me on top of him. At the same time, I couldn't let up. If I did, he could free his gun hand and pump me full of lead. This stalemate couldn't last. Something had to give.

And it did.

My knuckles were raw and bloody, as was the side of his head and ear, and that sound he kept making was really starting to get on my nerves. He got lucky, and his cast caught me a really smart one across the face, causing my vision to blur and me to bite my tongue. Unable to see, I misjudged a punch and threw a full-force haymaker into the floor, missing his head by inches. Instead of knocking him out, I'm pretty sure I broke a couple of knuckles.

This allowed him just enough space to wriggle under me and turn over. I was able to pin his gun hand to the ground with my left knee before he could bring it up. I was forced to bring up one arm to shield my face as the cast came back for my head. Balancing with my other hand, pinning his head, I started delivering vicious strikes with my right knee to his liver.

If you've never been struck in the liver, it's a fight-ender. Forget headshots. Ask any boxer, they'd take shots to the head all day rather than a single solid blow to the liver. It shuts your entire system down. I don't know if he just wasn't feeling pain for some reason or that, from my position, I wasn't able to generate enough power, rendering my hits as glancing blows, but he kept on wriggling.

One of his wild cast-punches went wide, under my blocking arm, and hit me...right in the nuts.

Forget that thing I just said about liver shots. Nut shots are a total system reboot.

Pain exploded low in my belly and radiated up into the back of my eyeballs until I could taste it. I could taste the pain. I felt like I was going to vomit as I involuntarily curled into a ball.

The fight was over. The guard struggled to his feet with a crazy smile on his face, still *ree*-ing like some deranged kid with emotional problems. He raised the Mac-10 as he stood over me.

Chapter 16

Shots rang out as I squeezed my eyes closed and waited to be torn in half by machine gunfire.

Something sounding a lot like a limp body hit the ground.

I opened my eyes, and the security guard was crumpled on the ground. As I slowly sat up, cradling my balls, the guard lay face down with five dark holes in the center of his back.

Alex came walking into my line of sight, still two-handing her little .38. Smoke curled out of the barrel like some old gunslinger western.

"You okay?"

I nodded in reply. I didn't exactly trust myself to speak without sounding like the mayor of Munchkin land.

She rolled the guard over and checked for a pulse. He was dead. He took five loads center-mass at close range. Not many people live through that.

Once my downstairs parts stopped responding with pain I experienced through multiple senses at once, I was able to gingerly get to my feet.

Staggering over to his body, I ran through his pockets, retrieving our guns, a can of lighter fluid, a lighter, and several empty magazines for the MAC-10. He'd been on his last mag. I took the MAC-10, ejected the mag, and topped it off with as many rounds as I could, taking 9mm rounds from Alex's Glock. I handed her the empty gun as well as my 1911, which was still loaded.

"What are you doing?" She took the guns.

"I got a bit of unfinished business to take care of." I loaded the now mostly full clip into the MAC-10 and pulled the bolt back. Flicking the safety on and switching it from full auto to semi, I swapped the gun over to my right hand and hefted it to my shoulder. I slipped the can of lighter fluid and lighter into my coat pocket.

"Okay, I'm coming with you."

"No, you're not," I told her, a hard, no-nonsense edge in my voice. "You're going to find a fire alarm, alert the police, and get out of the building. Do not argue with me."

She looked at me like she was seeing me for the first time. She didn't even try to argue. She did a press check on the Colt .45 to make sure it was loaded, and we headed for the elevators.

That's where we parted ways. I hit the up button on the elevator, and she made for the stairs.

As the doors opened to the lift, she called out. "Hey, Halson. Don't die."

I didn't even look at her. "I'm a Vampire Hunter. Death is what we do." I stepped in, and the doors slid closed.

I stood in the elevator as it went up, and an easy-listening Muzak version of "The Girl From Ipanema" started playing.

Ever notice how all elevators play that song? Like it's built into every single one of them by law.

I swayed with the music. Nothing wrong with boogieing down a little when you're walking into certain death.

When the elevator reached the floor and the doors opened, I held my breath.

The floor was dark like the others. The only light seemed to come from the lift. I stepped off carefully and into the lobby, keeping my eyes peeled for anything.

The old bat emerged from the dark, screaming like a banshee and going straight for my face. She didn't have a weapon and came at me with her nails like some kind of animal. Gone was the secretary's professional demeanor. Her once prim and proper, very definition of order and professionalism, was replaced by a woman possessed. Her suit dress was askew and her normally tight bun was coming undone in tangles. Her perfectly manicured hands were sharpened talons seeking any venerable flesh they could find. Going for my eyes or throat would've been lethal.

I didn't hesitate. I fired the MAC-10, putting one round in her gut and the second in her chest.

She collapsed like a scarecrow after a strong wind. Laying on the floor bleeding, she still spit and hissed at me like a cat.

I put the third round between her eyes and stepped over her body.

She must've been the vampire's thrall. Not my first time, but I hadn't suspected her until she attacked. Not once had I any reason to believe she'd been anything but a secretary. She'd been calm and collected, and perfectly put together the whole time I'd seen her prior. I'd never encountered a thrall that well put together. Usually, they were jabbering lunatics.

That said something about how strong the vampire had to be. Which didn't bode well for me. Older vampires are stronger.

They've had time to master and hone their powers. Once they reach about a hundred or so, they start to get into the really freaky ones, like hypnosis and mind control.

Thralls aren't in the same league, and younger vamps can make them, but they aren't exactly right. They're like crack addicts. All jittery and borderline insane, and the more thralls a young vampire makes, the more out of control they are. But a vamp with some decades and some practice under their belt can make thralls that are impossible to tell from regular humans. I wondered how many more there were.

I stepped around the buffer wall and into the long hallway that led to the executive offices. As I started down it, the hall suddenly twisted like a roller coaster. The ground beneath my feet swung back and forth as if I was on a rope bridge. Nausea and vertigo attacked me both at once. The walls started closing in on me, making me claustrophobic.

No, I told myself, do not panic. You are fine. It's just a psychic attack.

I tried to calm my mind with breathing exercises. Deep breath in, deep breath out. Repeat. It didn't help. I tried a bit of meditation. When that didn't help, I tried thinking about dead puppies and baseball.

I'd finally had enough. Taking the butt of the machine pistol, I smashed it into my nose until the pain made my eyes water. It hurt, and blood poured from my nose, but the hallway returned to normal, and the anxiety in my chest receded.

There's nothing like a bit of pain to reset the brain. I blinked tears from my eyes and continued down the hall to the door at the end.

The office door was a big, black hardwood. It loomed like a monolith. There was a brass plate set into it with a name. The words spiraled into meaninglessness. I shook my head, and the words returned to normal. *Victor Baptiste, President*, it read.

The man himself. The one behind the curtain pulling all the strings.

And one badass, powerful vampire. I took a deep breath and prepared to do battle.

I was essentially going in naked. I had none of my equipment or weapons. The only thing I was packing was what I'd taken off our homicidal little security guard. I was down to fighting a hundred year old crafty vampire with little more than a partially loaded machine pistol, a can of lighter fluid, a lighter, and some hurtful words.

Well, when you're royally screwed, things can't get worse, right?

I put my boot to the door and nearly broke my ankle. Hopping around on one foot for a few seconds, I checked the doorknob. It wasn't locked. I kicked the now-opened door. It swung inward, slamming against the wall and bouncing back until it clicked shut.

With my cool factor totally killed, I just opened the door like a normal person and shuffled in.

Baptiste stood behind his desk, facing away from the door and looking out the window. His tall, thin form was in stark contrast to light cast by a single desk light. The effect made him look inhumanly tall and skinny, making the Max Schrek comparison even more stark.

"Please, come in, Mr. Halson." His voice was deep and chilling. He was nailing the bad guy 101 tropes.

That just made me feel even more like a dope over my botched entry. At least no one was here to see it, and dead vampires can't tell on me.

"Yah know, I almost, for a second, didn't think it was you." I slowly moved around the room, the MAC held to my side and my other hand in my pocket on the can of lighter fluid. I tried to act casual, like I wasn't trapped in a cage with a hungry tiger who was thinking about ripping me apart. In stressful moments like this, it's really important to maintain the illusion of control and not pee your pants from fear.

"Oh, really?" he purred, still not bothering to turn and look at me. It's like he took classes or something.

"Yeah, when I saw you in Baker's office, you stood directly in the sunlight coming through the windows. I thought, well shit, he's not a vampire. And I got to say, it had me fooled. Until I figured out the glass in those windows contained a specialized coating that filtered out UV light. Then I knew it was you. I mean, you played it smart. You stayed behind the scenes. You didn't directly interact with the investigation or investigators. You kept a buffer between yourself and the police."

I kept babbling. My plan was simple: get close, throw lighter fluid on him, and then light him up. If I was quick and lucky, it might work. My ass might also sprout wings and fly me to the moon, too. "But you made mistakes."

"Oh, and what mistakes were those?"

Still nothing, no reaction. I might as well have been a fly with much attention as he paid me. He was really playing the role hard. Either he was committed to the villain bit, or he'd forgotten how to be human. It happens. When you live long enough with nothing to fear, and live off the lives and suffering of others, you tend to go a little screwy and forget your humanity. The ego seems to be the first thing to go haywire after a vampire starts to gain a little bit of power. Or maybe megalomaniacs just take to being a monster quicker.

"Yeah, you sicced your pet beastie on my friend, killing him. Then you sent your goon after me, and he killed a nice little old lady whose one crime was being in my employ. That was a mistake, because now I'm going to kill you."

"I assure you, Mr. Curly was not my 'goon' as you call him."

Holy crap. His name was Curly. So many missed *Three Stooges* jokes.

"He was operating solely on his hatred of you."

I shrugged. "I have that effect on people."

"Clearly. For example, I want to rip your guts out. I find that a far more amusing prospect rather than letting you prattle on."

"Bring it, you Christoper Lee wannabe. But answer me one thing." I stalled. I wasn't yet close enough. Just a couple more steps, and I would be close enough to splash him. "Why did you kill Baker in such a public way?"

He laughed, finally showing some kind of emotion other than boredom. "I would've thought that was obvious. Confusion." He stroked his chin in classic villain cliché fashion. "Donald found out about how I fund my lifestyle. Modern times are so convenient. Did you know I'm almost two hundred years old?"

Crap.

"Yes, things used to be difficult, selecting, stalking, and then killing people. You had to be very careful, and it was so inefficient. Killing every couple of days and trying to keep from alerting people. Disposing of bodies and covering up murders. Constantly on the move. Then, times changed. Cities got bigger and denser, and humanity became more and more apathetic. And you have no idea how great the medical advances have made things. Blood collection and donation, disease screenings. Now, I have a steady supply of untraceable food that no one would investigate."

"Except Baker," I interrupted him, waxing poetic about the good old days as I slid closer while trying to make it look like I wasn't trying to get closer.

"Yes, though it was really my fault. It's these computers. I can't seem to get the hang of them. Some features of the system let him see when I changed the finance numbers to cover the blood bank costs. Making all that blood vanish without a trace isn't cheap. He thought I was embezzling from the company, and more importantly, from him. He tried to blackmail me with threats to the FTC unless he got his cut. There was no cut to be had, and that money solely existed for my private stocks. He thought he had me over a barrel." A smile touched his undead lips, making him look even more like Count Olaf.

"He didn't know you were a vampire."

"No, he did not." His grin grew wider. "He was surprised by my counteroffer. And by that, I mean I had him drained of his blood. Waste not, want not."

"Why throw him out the window? Why not just make him disappear?"

"I thought about that, but I had to get rid of the body, and he had already been missing for several days by that point. People were asking questions. He was skipping meetings, and then the accounting department sent notice of questionable discrepancies in the books. The whole thing was coming apart, so I had to muddy the waters. I threw poor Donald out his window and let the police do the hard part for me. My plan worked brilliantly. By making it look like a fake vampire attack, they would waste time trying to find a real vampire while all the clues lead them in the wrong direction. I didn't think they would bring in a real vampire hunter, but I felt secure that the obvious fakery would make them take the case less seriously. It was beautiful. My plan worked perfectly until you wouldn't leave like you were supposed to. So, I had to give you a real vampire to hunt. I'd hoped the Nosferatu would kill you, but it got the cop instead. Pity, it was a neat little bow on the package, but Mr. Curly screwed things up. He got so fixated on you that he started running around, getting in my way. I should've killed him rather than fired him. Que sera, sera, I guess. In the end, it all worked out."

I burst out laughing, and that finally got the vampire to turn around and look at me with a shocked expression.

"Seriously? That was you master plan? That's not a plan, that's...that's just *stupid*!"

He frowned and growled at me. He actually growled.

"What did you say, you little worm?" Baptiste snarled, baring his fangs. His perfect Crest white teeth were gone, replaced by craggy, yellowed things that lay in blackened gums with long sharp points.

"That's not a plan, that's dumb. It's something a hack writer comes up with on the fly when he's on a publishing deadline." I kept laughing, holding my side. "Holy shit, man. That was some Looney Tunes stuff. That *plan* has so many things that could've gone wrong, and relied on way too many things going right. You could've just made Baker vanish and blame the embezzling on him. Pretend he went on the run when the accounting firm found the errors. It would've been a lot less work and so much easier to pull off."

Apparently, Baptiste's ego couldn't handle being laughed at. Either due to years of being in the corporate world or decades of being a vampire, or someone he saw as his inferior coming up with such an obvious plan he hadn't thought of, pushed his buttons. His eyes blazed as the pupils grew, devouring the whites of his eyes until even the sclera was black.

"You don't get it." He hissed. "You are just too unintelligent to see how masterful my plan was." From deep inside the black pits of his eyes came a red glow like campfire embers.

"Oh, no. I can clearly see how dumb it was." I chuckled, loving that this was getting to him. "You just bet against me being stupid. Never bet against me being stupid."

I went to make my move, but as my hand cleared my pocket, popping the top on the lighter fluid, he blinked.

Chapter 17

I don't mean his eyes blinked. He vanished, except he didn't. He just kinda moved so fast, my eyes couldn't track him. It was like when watching a film, and it skipped a couple of frames. One second, he was in front of me, the next, he was behind me.

His long-fingered hand clamped onto the back of my neck like an iron manacle. The next thing I knew, the office room was shooting away from me as he threw me, one-handed, backward into the office wall. I went through the faux woodwork and into the next room.

It was an east-facing conference room of some kind. The long conference table caught me around mid-thigh, and I went sliding the entire length of it before toppling off the other end and onto the floor. So fast, my body didn't even register the pain. I just kinda flopped around on the floor like a fish trying to get my limbs to work. It would have been comical if I hadn't been in danger.

By the time I managed to shake off most of the whiplash, Baptiste was making his way slowly, methodically across the room. He had to duck low to get through the hole I made when I went through the wall, but he did it with liquid grace. His tall, spindly body moved like a dancer, smooth practiced grace and fluid motions.

I braced myself as he blinked across the room again. He was instantly in front of me and gave me a one-handed shove. I flew back into the conference room wall with bone-jarring force, but not enough to send me through it. My back teeth came loose, though. Somehow, I managed to get my legs under me before I hit the floor. Using the wall, I found myself in a sort of quasi-crouch. I couldn't do much except bring my arms up to shield my head as the vampire blinked again.

Baptiste swatted me with one of his spider-like hands. He was so fast and strong, I found myself flying sideways along the wall after that hit. Not sure if he was pulling his punches to enjoy the suffering or just not getting the right angle to kill me, but as I struck the third wall, I was seriously starting to think about changing my business cards to "Tobias Halson: Professional Pinball."

The impact this time was less, and I pushed off the wall, taking a half-assed fighter's stance. I still had the MAC-10 in one hand, but there was no chance I was gonna be able to use it on him. Not while he was mind-freaking me so he could hop around and throw sucker punches.

I was ready this time when he blinked. I threw a punch where I knew he was going to be. I must have miscalculated, or he saw it coming, because he popped up about six inches to the left of my punch. There was no time to react before he kicked me in the gut, sending me crashing up into the ceiling like a hacky sack.

My insides were on fire and the breath whooshed from my lungs.

I fell in slow motion. I had plenty of time to watch the floor come up to catch me as my brain started working overtime, sensing death around the corner. Yeah, I was down. This was the final count.

Remember in *Rocky* how he lost the fight, and what a bummer that was? That's basically what I was looking at here. Except there was no feel good moral victory, just a slow painful death.

I hoped Alex had gotten out and managed to contact the police.

I had lost all sense of time from the beatings and concussions. I had no clue what time it was until I lifted my head. From under the conference table, the horizon glowed in red and yellow as the sun rose. It caused shadows in the office to stretch lazily across the room in long dark bars cast by the table and chair legs.

Oh, great. At least I got to see one more sunrise. Got to say, it was beautiful. The shadows shifted as the sun came up slowly, moving like the hands of a clock counting down my last seconds alive.

Wait a minute.

I had an idea, but I was only going to get one shot at it. If my guess was correct, then I knew how he was doing the blinking thing. It was his eyes. When I'd caught a glimpse of them, he must've been hypnotizing me. He wasn't moving fast. He was causing me to freeze for a few seconds.

I slowly managed to get to my feet. I had barely enough strength to stand. I wasn't going to get a second shot at this. I kept my gaze down, looking at the shadows on the floor, watching for the subtle jump in time to test my theory. If I didn't meet his eyes, I would be fine.

With each breath, I ignored the pain, sharpened my focus, and waited for my moment.

The vampire's long, black shadow swept across the floor toward me. It was fast, but not like instant teleportation. There was no time skip this time. The shadows didn't suddenly leap forward, and I knew I could pull it off.

Without looking, I threw the can of lighter fluid in his direction. As if on instinct, it caught the can in one long-fingered hand. Without missing a beat or lifting my eyes, I fired the MAC-10, putting a round not through the vampire, but through the can of lighter fluid. It exploded from the force and doused him in flammable liquid.

"Burn, baby, burn," I said as I pulled the zippo from my coat pocket and flicked it open in one deft move. I thumbed the striker and...nothing. I flicked it again. Still nothing.

Oh, mother fu—

He laughed and smacked the lighter from my hand. My arm went numb up to my elbow.

"Is that it? Is that all you have, mighty Vampire Hunter?" He threw back his head and laughed.

"I have a machine gun. Ho, ho, ho."

Baptiste must not have been a big movie watcher, as that seemed to confuse him.

I flipped the switch on the MAC from semi to full-auto and lifted it. Holding the gun sideways, gangster style, I squeezed the trigger, allowing the recoil to drag the muzzle from right to left, spraying the whole room with gunfire. This was an old WWII shooting technique developed by Chinese resistance fighters to assassinate Japanese occupation forces. It's a pretty nasty little trick. They would pop into bars and offices, use the shooting technique to spray the room, and then take off, leaving a room full of corpses behind. It was so devastating, the Japanese came to fear it and called it "bandit shooting."

Of course, it works a hell of a lot better on people than vampires.

Baptiste dropped the arm he'd used to shield himself. The measly handful of rounds he'd taken had done nothing to him.

He grinned that sadistic smile again, his fangs long and gleaming like ivory.

"Did you think that would stop me, foolish mortal?"

Oh, he was getting into it now. I was feeling a thee or thou coming any second.

I glared at him. "No, but then again, I wasn't aiming for you."

His expression fell into confusion again. I was really starting to vex him. The vampire had no counter measure for my cartoonish antics or ADHD-like hair-brained schemes. There was no way for him to begin to comprehend my tactics unless he'd spent the last hundred years watching *Looney Toons*. He had no idea I was going Wile E. Coyote all over his Road Runner ass.

He finally noticed what I was looking at, and followed my gaze over his shoulder.

The entire outside wall of the conference room was floor-to-ceiling windows, meant to let in as much sunlight as possible. Just like in Baker's office, they were the special UV-treated windows. Which meant the sunlight coming through the glass didn't affect Baptiste.

However, now there were dozens of neat little round bullet holes all along the windows. As the sun rose and shone through, the holes let in beams of unfiltered light that crisscrossed the whole room in a network of lethal sunlight

Still confused, he looked down at one such beam that hit his arm where a bullet had ripped through the lighter fluid-soaked sleeve of his suit. His eyes went wide a second before his skin caught fire. The flames rapidly spread over his body as his expensive suit, soaked in flammable liquid, fully engulfed him.

With a confused roar, he turned on me and lunged with his mouth open tond fangs bared. I was expecting him, though. And as fast as he was, he wasn't supernaturally quick. I reached up and caught one fang between my thumb and forefinger on each hand. Flames licked at my arms from his burning body.

"Yippee-Ki-Yay, bloodsucker!" I'd always wanted to use the *Die Hard* line, and I snapped his fangs off at the gums.

I raised a boot and kicked him in the chest. I don't know if he was trying to flee, lost his sense of direction, or my kick was just that strong, but the vampire slammed through the fractured glass of one of the windows and into open space. He plummeted thirty stories to the pavement below, a howling ball of fire.

He hit the ground as a twisted bundle of burning clothes and sticks as the flames peeled away his flesh. Even from that high up, I could hear his final screams as they petered out in the morning air.

It was sometime later I managed to find my way downstairs with the help of some kindly EMTs and their wonderful stretcher. On the way down, the elevator played "The Girl from Ipanema."

Every freaking time.

Chapter 18

The building didn't burn down. Pity.

Curly had only managed to disable the sprinklers on that one floor, and the closet fire had snuffed itself out when it ran out of oxygen. We still would've died if we hadn't gotten out of there.

Alex had evacuated everyone else in the building after pulling the alarm. She'd even managed to call in police backup. It was a shame they only arrived in time to witness Baptiste's swan dive out the window.

The papers were going nuts over the whole thing. Rumors were flying everywhere, from Enon-like Ponzi schemes to police cover-ups. Someone even told a story about vampire blood banks, but that article quickly devolved into antisemitic tropes and neo-Nazi stuff, so no one took it seriously. That was, sadly, the closest anyone got to the real truth.

My injuries were mainly superficial. A fractured hand and broken nose were about the worst of it. The doctors kept going on about brain injuries, but no one really needs one of those, right? Despite spending the next week smelling the color purple, I was absolutely pineapple.

The funerals were the horrible part. I went with Alex to Bullard's. It was pretty nice. He had a big turnout. His friends, family, and cop buddies all showed up. He even got a twenty-one gun salute, and a gold pocket watch to signal the end of his watch.

Cops are a little morbid.

The worst part was seeing his family. I hung back and watched from the edge of the crowd. His wife cried the whole time, but it was his son that got to me. The little kid looked just like his dad, except for his eyes. Bullard's eyes, even when gentle or intense, always had a spark of life to them. Warmth. Like the man saw through all of life's misery and pain and kept on trucking because it was all worth it. Even at his most hard and cynical, it was there. After all, the eyes are the windows to the soul.

Bullard's kid's eyes, at maybe seven or eight years old, looked familiar. They were flat and cold and burned with an inner fire that threatened to consume everything around him. I saw those eyes quite a lot. Every time I looked in the mirror, in fact.

A friend once told me that they looked upon my soul and saw a deep ocean of sadness, but below those depths was a deeper, darker trench where something monstrous lurked. Looking at that kid, I think I understood what they meant.

Bullard's son didn't cry, not once. Not even when his mother fell to pieces on his tiny shoulders. He now carried on those shoulders the weight of the world and the legacy of his father, who he would struggle to match up to for the rest of his life. That shadow would loom over him as he grew into manhood, just itching for his shot at revenge.

One day, just maybe, someone like me would come knocking on his door and offer him that chance.

Alex didn't cry. But then again, I couldn't tell. It was raining, and everyone was soaked. She looked good in her police blues. Very professional. But beyond standing next to me, she barely acknowledged me, as if she was distancing herself from me in front of all her police colleagues.

I got it. She didn't want to be associated with me, even in front of the other losers. Bullard was a big man, and no one talked shit to him, about him, or behind his back. But Alex wasn't him. She wasn't imposing enough to instill fear or intimidation into the rest of them. Nor did she have enough experience to inspire them to rally around her leadership. On top of that, she was a woman—a woman in a man's job.

Sexism, one of the world's many problems.

It was going to be bad for her for a while, and it was probably better she not be seen with me for a bit.

She did show up to Anita's funeral. It was very different. Bullard's had been grand and fancy with an expensive coffin and tons of mourners, and a big headstone paid for by the city. Anita's was much sadder. It was just the two of us. A small plot of land in the cemetery with a modest headstone. I had sprung for the nicest one I could afford, but the insurance money from the office didn't pay out much, and what was left, I sent to her family.

I should've kept it since none of them bothered to show up. She'd been a great lady and a bigger part of my life than I'd realized. The world felt emptier without her in it. Colors weren't as bright, food didn't taste as good, and birds didn't even sing. It wasn't fair. Why did such a good person have to lose everything while people like me kept on going?

Families and lives had been destroyed, and for me, it was just Tuesday. Times like this, I think I'm not cut out for this kinda thing. It would be easier if I just cut out everyone and everything, and go solo. Fewer people would get hurt, and there would be fewer funerals. I wouldn't have to see the looks on faces when you told them their loved ones were dead. Not having to see that flash of anger in their eyes as they thought, why them? Why not you? Why did my spouse or loved one have to die when no one would've missed you?

I spiraled into my dark thoughts as they lowered her casket in the ground. I wondered how many people would attend my funeral. Who would? Would Alex? Or would she already be dead? Another victim in my wake. Would I even get a funeral, or would I just be dead in a ditch somewhere? A fitting end to a lifetime of causing misery.

I think about that winter's night years ago and the scents, the wonderful memories of Christmas, and wish I'd died with my family that night. Then maybe all this suffering wouldn't have happened.

But, the monsters, Tobias. What about the monsters? My Uncle Dale's voice was in my head. What about all the people who would've died if not for the vampires you've slain?

Yes, I had done good in the world, but did that outweigh the bad? Was it enough to balance the scales?

I didn't know. Those were the questions that kept me up at night. Thinking black thoughts as I held my father's gun and contemplated taking the coward's way out. How could anyone, anyone drowning in this much death and pain, be a coward? Who could fault them for running away? After everything, didn't I deserve some peace, too? To not feel like a piece of shit every time I walked away after shattering someone's life?

How much death could one person stand?

Alex's hand slipped into mine as we stood grave side. When she squeezed my hand, it made me feel a little better. Like maybe, just maybe, I could keep going. Just a little longer.

After all, I'm a Vampire Hunter.

Death is what we do.

Afterword

The "Tobias Halson Hunter" series, especially this book, has a troubled past. The version here is very different from how it started out. This book was one of the ones I was in the middle of working on in the early 2010s when I had a serious laptop failure. This was before I had cloud storage or any kind of real backup system. It was all pretty much on my computer when it failed. I ended up losing a lot of work. The original first draft of "Midnight Falls" was the biggest casualty as I was never able to recover more than the Prologue. I was a bit more lucky with the "Halson" books. I managed to recover most of what I had at the time, save a chapter or two, looking through old website accounts and thumb drives.

Escaping the ether wasn't the only issue the book faced. About two-thirds through, somewhere around the Nosferatu attack in the basement, I had an idea for the sequel. Having a head full of ADHD-riddled brain goblins meant I had to immediately chase this new shiny thing. It's a fairly common occurrence for writers. We joke about it, but it's a real thing. New ideas are exciting, whereas projects that have made it over the third chapter hump, the bloom has gone off the rose.

I ended up finishing the sequel before I finished the first book. Talk about putting the cart before the horse. But in doing so, the character of Tobias Halson changed completely. In my original manuscript, Tobais was an older angrier character. More of a 40s Noir detective. Think Sam Spade, but with a touch of *Buffy the Vampire Slayer*. He was a lot gruffer, sexist, misogynistic, homophobic, generally an unlikable asshole character along the lines of Gregory House. This was intentional as I'd planned to redeem the character over the course of the series.

Some people have cited *Harry Dresden* as the inspiration for this character, and I do love Jim Butcher's work, but the actual inspiration was Laurell K Hamilton's *Anita Blake*.

The Anita Blake character is very interesting in that she starts out as your typical hypocritical Midwestern conservative. She is an angry bigot, close-minded to anything that challenges her preconceived notions, and clings to a religion that actively hates her for who and what she is as a circumstance of birth. It's only through prolonged forced interaction with the marginalized communities she'd despised did she eventually become deprogrammed and become open-minded, leading to a journey of self-discovery, and to become a better person. The series as a whole is a fairly interesting analogy for LGBTQ+ and marginalized communities, and how just by engaging and understanding them undermines the hate and lies of bigotry.

I wanted to do something similar with Halson, minus getting sidetracked by ten volumes of vetting sexual frustration until the fan base had all but jumped ship.

However, in writing the sequel first, the character changed due to the interactions with another character, Gillette. You'll meet him in the sequel, and will either love him or want to punch him in the face. The chemistry between the two was more 80s buddy cop and comedic lending a softer, more humanized tone to the character. I went with it because I found myself liking the guy. So, when I came back to this one, I made him more likable. In the first version, he was meaner, and came across as more shell-shocked due to his traumatic past, taking it out on others with snark that boarded on just being pointlessly mean.

The new version was more sad suffering from survivor's guilt and turning his anger inwards toward himself with his social awkwardness manifesting as snark, in a reflection of my own. This made the character a lot more Buffy than Spade, and I ran with it, liking how the new version handled the same events in a much different manner. While both versions handle most problems in a combative nature, the first was a lot more *Punisher*. Where violence wasn't the answer, it was the question, and the answer was "yes, and lots of it." The revamped (pun) Halson is more *Deadpool*, cracking jokes and escaping by the skin of his teeth while breaking the fourth wall and pretending it all went to plan.

While I missed out on my idea of redeeming an unlikable character, I ended up with something fun that I liked. That is really what the Halson books are about: me having fun.

When I write my short stories, I'm experimenting. Trying out new things and formats and attempting to improve myself as a writer. While writing my horror novels, I'm more serious and trying to see how far I've come as a writer. I play the Halson books more fast and loose. They're just me having fun and making myself laugh. Not to say I don't enjoy writing the other stuff, I do. It's just that the Halson books are about making myself laugh, and taking my mind off things.

It's also why they're a bit shorter than my other stuff. They are meant to be fast and snappy, and readers these days tend to enjoy having some shorter form stuff as opposed to behemoth books clocking in at more than 150k words.

Of course, this cavalier attitude does have its downside. When it came time to publish the Halson series, I kinda misplaced the manuscript. Which meant a panicked three week search through every storage device and backup I have while promising my publisher I wasn't the idiot screw up I clearly appeared to be. It's not that I'm messy and disorganized, it's just that I practice chaotic order. Everything may look messy, but I swear I know exactly where everything is. It just looks like utter chaos to an outsider. There is a method to my madness, even if I don't know what it is.

It was a bit of a wakeup call, honestly. If I was gonna take this writer thing seriously, I was going to have to shape up and try to keep things organized. Which lead to a complete overhaul of how I store my manuscripts and copies. Hopefully this doesn't happen in the future, or my publisher is gonna have my hide. They had to wait over a month for me to find the final draft (at least, I hope it was the final draft) of the sequel manuscript. And as of writing this, they are still waiting for the rough draft of "A Mothers Rage" I promised them last December.

I don't know how that woman puts up with me...or any woman, for that matter.

I'm happy the Halson series is finally going into print. I'm not trying to take the Urban Fantasy genre by storm or anything. I'm just having fun and hoping you do, too. If you enjoy this one, check out the sequel "Werewolf Hunter."

CHECK OUT THESE OTHER GREAT READS FROM ROWAN PROSE:

John Evans is the author of the pulse-pumping book "Midnight Falls." He also writes the "Tobias Halson Hunter" urban fantasy series and various short stories. Inspired by greats like Stephen King and Gary Brandner, he loves all things "old school" horror, and often claims his purpose is to give readers a little bit of fun Lovecraftian escapism from the scarier real world.

www.ingramcontent.com/pod-product-compliance
Lightning Source LLC
Chambersburg PA
CBHW020804310726
48969CB00002B/687